Lebo Mazibuko

Bantu Knots

Kwela Books

Kwela Books,
an imprint of NB Publishers,
a division of Media24 Boeke (Pty) Ltd
40 Heerengracht, Cape Town, South Africa
PO Box 879, Cape Town, South Africa, 8000
www.kwela.com

Copyright © 2021 Lebohang Mazibuko

Cover design by publicide
Typography by Nazli Jacobs
Set in Palatino

Printed by **novus print**, a division of Novus Holdings

First edition, first impression 2021
Second impression 2023

ISBN: 978-0-7957-1027-8

To my mother and father,
thank you for giving me the space to pursue all that is
in my heart. Your support has been my strength.

DINEO

Kwasukasukela

Once upon a time

My grandmother pulled me out of bed. My eyes were still half shut as I sleepily scrambled on the floor in search of my slippers.

'Come.'

Before I could reach them, she yanked me from the floor and pulled me outside.

I shivered, my toes numbing as my feet sank into the cold soil.

'Lift up your nightdress,' my grandmother ordered, clutching a broom in her hand.

I tucked my fingers under my knee-high nightdress and pulled it all the way up to my chin. She took the broom and swept it over my flat chest. She brushed over each nipple with precision. I stood quietly, feeling the rough bristles on the tenderness of my chest. The full moon was still sitting pretty in the sky. Soon, its radiance would be dimmed by the rising sun.

'It's early – you can go back to bed. But clean your feet first.'

I headed for the bathroom and poured water into the basin.

I took the greyish stone that my grandmother used to soften her calluses and scrubbed off the dirt before returning to bed.

* * *

I sank my body into the water, my head stroking the surface. Eyes shut, I drifted into nothingness. When I dried myself, my chest felt unfamiliar to my touch. I touched again. My nipples had grown larger and thicker. They were darker in colour, protruding more than they had before. When I pressed and poked them, they felt like two large nuts.

She had swept over them during the last full moon. Whatever my grandmother's intentions – to make my breasts grow or, more likely, to stop them from growing – my breasts began growing at a pace which was noticeably faster than that of the rest of the girls in my class.

That morning, I was anxious to get to school. I needed to tell someone. My only friend at school was Sindiswa – Sindi, for short. I pulled her into the toilet cubicle during break-time and lifted my tunic.

'Sheba,' I whispered, showing her my little secret.

Sindi prodded and gently squeezed my small cone-shaped nipples. 'Ngempela ayakhula. Yoh, you actually have real breasts now, Naledi.'

She started thinking of ways to ask her mother to sweep over her flat chest.

'It wasn't my mother, Sindi. It was my grandmother,' I explained.

'Oh, so it has to be uGogo who sweeps over them?'

8

'Ya, otherwise I don't think they will grow.'

'Yoh mara uGogo uhlala eMlazi. How and when will I get to Umlazi to my grandmother?'

'You'll have to wait, I guess.'

'Until June holidays, Naledi? Yoh haa, I can't wait; phela I'm getting older every day. I'm older than you – nearly thirteen,' she protested.

Sindi and I pondered for a moment before Sindi jumped up into the air in excitement, remembering what having breasts meant for a girl.

'Hawu we ma, so you are going to start wearing bras, Naledi?'

I beamed, imagining the snug cupped material holding together my womanly assets. We ran out of the girls' toilets giggling, to gorge on our packed lunches.

In class I didn't focus much. I was too busy dreaming about the day I would go bra shopping for the first time. What sort of panties would I get to go along with my bras? Would I buy those three-in-a-pack panties like I had always done, or would I finally get the single panties that sit pretty on a hanger? Would I start matching my bras with my panties and when was the decent age for a girl to start wearing G-strings?

'Naledi!' my teacher shouted. My body jolted.

'Keng nkare o robetse! Are you listening?'

Everyone was staring at me. I was being reprimanded. I never got reprimanded. I always listened, kept quiet in class and worked diligently.

When the school bell rang, I couldn't get out of class fast

enough. Sindi found me waiting for her at the gate. We would usually walk home together and part ways halfway between my house and her house. That afternoon we had an in-depth discussion about Minenhle's hair. Minenhle was the pastor's daughter who had the prestigious task of reading out the announcements before the close of service. Sindi and I were in awe of Minenhle's beauty and eloquence. Even more impressive was how long her ponytail was. My little bantu knots and Sindi's short afro were no match for Minenhle's straight long pushback that could be tied into a phondo. Her ponytail would move in the opposite direction when she turned her head. And on those occasional Sundays when Minenhle would let her hair loose, her raven hair would flow elegantly down her nape, kissing her shoulders.

'Ngithi, even when she walks, iphondo lakhe, it swings from side to side. And uyazi ke, a girl like that will never tell anyone what she relaxes her hair with,' Sindi went on. She paused, then in a burst of passion said, 'Dark and Lovely! It must be it. But the one that has uNonhle Thema on the box, not the one with the little girl.'

'Haa, no, Sindi, it can't be. Her head would burn if she used that. That one is for grown-ups.'

'Oho ke wena, have you tried it?'

'No, I still use Beautiful Beginnings, the one for kids.'

'Uyabona ke, Naledi, that's why your hair is growing so slow. And worse njalo, you are always plaiting and twisting your hair into these funny popcorn knots. And these things eat away your hair if you didn't know.'

Sindi was a fine one to talk, considering that my hair was much longer than hers. I was well on my way to getting my hair to where Minenhle's hair was – my mother was making sure of that. How could Sindi have all these facts and ideas about growing hair when her mother refused for her to put any chemical in her hair to begin with? She told me herself that chemicals made her hair fall out.

When we reached our halfway point, we said goodbye and I walked down to the Somalian man's shop to buy myself a kota. I had waited on purpose for Sindi to leave because I didn't want to have to share it. I deserved a really good one – I had saved up for two weeks for this kota.

Instead of studying, I sat at the kitchen table at home with my books open in front of me, guzzling my russian, polony, cheese, chips and atchar-filled bread. My grandmother's arrival at six woke me up – I had fallen asleep with my head on my books. There was no greeting, just the usual question about my mother's whereabouts.

I told her that I had no idea, and as usual she sucked her teeth. 'Mxm.'

My grandmother and I both knew very well that my mother was either out with her best friend *looking for a man* or she was *with a man*. With the air turned sour from the question, Mama, the name I called my grandmother, went on to prepare dinner. I saw more of my grandmother than I did my mother, so I called her 'Mama' and my mother by name. Mama and I sat quietly at the kitchen table to partake of our meal: morogo, wors and pap.

'Naledi,' my grandmother said, before adding with careful intent, 'a girl oils her body and spirit in sin when she spreads her legs for a man before he marries her. A punishable act in the eyes of God. Do you hear me?'

'Yes, Mama.' I nodded, and we continued to eat in silence.

My grandmother always made it a point to remind me of the many things that God hated and sent people to Hell for. I feared going to Hell. I feared being engulfed by flames for all eternity. So during our nightly prayer, I asked God to forgive me for not concentrating in class earlier but instead daydreaming about buying G-strings and bras. I asked God to forgive me for coveting Minenhle's hair and for good measure I also asked Him to forgive me for not wanting to share my kota with Sindi. I promised Him to be better and not to oil my body in sin like my mother was doing. I assured God that I would do everything in my power to keep as far away as possible from boys.

* * *

Staying away from mischievous behaviour was difficult, especially on a Saturday when so much always happened on Ndende Street. As if pulled by a magnet, I would find myself standing by the gate with envious eyes watching the kids whom my grandmother had forbidden me from playing with running around with empty cans and an old stocking playing chigago and mogusha.

I would have been in very big trouble with my grandmother if she caught me outside at the gate just before midday. *'The fool folds his hands and consumes his own flesh,'* she would say.

But the drama that seemed to follow the grown-ups who lived on our street was even more entertaining than watching soapies.

Like Bra Joe and Sis' Nozipho. The couple had only been married for a few months. Mama had been there at Bra Joe's house chopping onions and peeling potatoes with the other women from our community while the men slaughtered a cow and brewed umqombothi at the back of the house. All this happened while my mother and I stood in the yard with Bra Joe's family singing 'Ntab' ezikude we ma zingisithela wena' across the locked gate, Sis' Nozipho outside the gate covered in a blanket surrounded by her chorusing family. Bra Joe's uncle had kept the keys in his hands, refusing to let Sis' Nozipho and her family in until they gave a satisfactory performance, and the battle had continued until after midnight.

The next afternoon had been a sea of colour – from the brightly dressed people to the seven-coloured food. It was amazing how that cow managed to feed all the people who overflowed from the white tent they had pitched in the middle of our street. There was i-step, which consisted of just a few simple moves that the wedding party had choreographed, but nothing gets people excited like watching people dance. I stayed out till late, until Sis' Nozipho was brought, with a kist at her side, into her new home. That's how Zulu people say, 'till death do us part' – you come as a bride into your new home with a box and you will only leave that home in a box.

Now, watching Bra Joe being locked out of his yard and Sis' Nozipho holding the keys and refusing to let him in was funny. The past Wednesday had been the 25th of the month and also Bra Joe's pay day. Bra Joe did what he always did on the Friday after the 25th – he stayed out all night getting drunk with his boys at a nearby shisa nyama.

'Vula le gate maan. Nozipho, open up!' he shouted, loudly enough for me to hear him four gates away.

'Ngithe hamba – go back to where you came from!' Sis' Nozipho retorted from inside her yard that had a big painted board on her face-brick wall with the words 'Nozipho's Hair Salon' sprayed on it.

'This is my house! You won't lock me out of my own house. Vula maan, Nozipho!'

Bra Joe was in the same clothes that I had seen him wearing the previous morning. His white shirt was hanging out of his brown chinos and his usually sleek pomaded haircut was in need of some fresh gel and a brush.

'Uyang'jwayela wena! Where did you sleep last night, nobani futhi?' Sis' Nozipho interrogated Bra Joe.

'Hayi maan, Nozipho, open up this gate!' Bra Joe yelled, holding the bars of the gate and shaking them.

Karabo from next door, who I viewed more as my big sister than anything else, was dressed in her nightdress and doek, when she returned from the shop. For most girls around here, taking a bath before going to the shops really wasn't a big deal. Nobody cared except for my grandmother, who wouldn't let me dare leave the yard in my nightie.

Karabo pulled one legwinya out of her bag. 'Come, tshwara. I know you want one.'

Karabo was well aware of my weaknesses: kgogo ya Sesotho, cooked by her mother, and magwinya le snoek fish, the traditional kasi Saturday breakfast. She knew I could not say no. I ran towards her and stuck my hand through the fence to accept it.

'I'll see you later, neh,' Karabo said. I gulped down the warm deep-fried fat cake before my grandmother caught sight of it. It sat very pleasantly in my belly and affirmed my decision to stand around outside.

I thanked God for Karabo: not only did she sneak me treats but she was the one person around Zone 2 I could talk to, usually through the wire fence that separated our two homes. Karabo was very petite, with a dry-curl hairdo under her doek. I think I envied her as much as I admired her. I certainly hoped that one day I too would walk with my shoulders back, head held high, with an unmistakable yet subtle shifting of my butt with each step.

Her company was even better than the sway in her hips. She was smart and always knew just what to say.

A whistle pulled my attention away from Karabo. 'Hey, Mnyamane,' the man said to me. It was Xolani – the man believed to be my father, though he had for twelve years vehemently denied this ever to be true. He still spoke proudly of having slept with my mother at a street bash all those years ago. But Xolani was also sure to remind everyone that my mother had in fact been seventeen and not a virgin and he had been almost thirty when all of this had occurred. 'Loose' and 'fast' are the terms he used to describe my mother. My mother made many tongues wag wherever she went, for both her beauty and her indiscretions. I couldn't wait for the day that I would finally stop hearing about this nauseating story. Neither Xolani nor my mother had seemed to get over it.

Perhaps it was time for me to learn how to pray in tongues because my basic prayers in Setswana to make all this stop were clearly not working. The ability to pray in tongues was next-level praying. Everyone in our church knew that such prayers moved the hand of God. And I desperately needed God to help me deal with Xolani. But the only twelve-year-old I knew who could pray in tongues was Minenhle. Mama and everyone in our church had been blown away when Minenhle had stood in the pulpit and allowed her tongue to roll in a language none of us could interpret.

Xolani was sitting with two younger men, Clement and Thabiso, on an old car seat outside the fence of the house directly across the street. He was holding a beer bottle.

'Ja, Mnyamane,' he repeated. 'You don't look like your mother, but I can tell by your big butt and hips that you're her child.'

'Eh, ja mara baby girl opakile yeses, she has one of those bums that you can see from the front,' Thabiso added.

'Motho o ke ngwana bafwethu, leave her alone,' said Clement, trying to defend my honour.

Thabiso practically lived across the street at Clement's mother's house. No one was really sure exactly where Thabiso had come from, but what everyone knew was that ever since Thabiso had arrived, all he and Clement seemed to do was to

16

sit under the tree, smoke cigarettes and drink, talking about soccer, politics, parties and girls.

'Ja mara eish, look at her properly, Clemza. Really look at her and you'll see what we are talking about,' Thabiso said.

All three pairs of eyes immediately began to remove each inch of my yellow dress, dropping it to the floor. They peeled away every layer and undergarment I was wearing. I felt a flush of shame shooting through my body. I hoped that they wouldn't notice my protruding nipples.

'O kae Mme wa hao wa sefebe? Tell her I'm not your father,' Xolani said before taking a gulp of his beer. He then turned back to the others: 'You know, that bitch says I'm this child's father, ungijwayela amasimba le cherrie. Phela, I went in with a condom – you can't just go in there without strapping.' Traces of spit flew from his lips whenever he pronounced his consonants.

'Ja vele ons weet – we all know her here. She's a walking STD that one,' Clement said.

I began to walk backwards, taking very slow steps. I knew that if I turned around too soon they would zero in on my butt again. When I felt safe, I turned around and ran to the back of the house, behind the outdoor toilet. I curled up in a ball and shoved my head between my knees.

Once I'd stopped crying, I began to remove all evidence of sobbing. I didn't want my grandmother to ask me too many questions. I stood up, lifting up the bottom part of my dress, I used it to wipe away my tears. I then looked down at myself, scrutinising my body. I touched my thighs, then placed my hand on my belly. I touched each mark and poked each dimple. I turned my head to peek at my butt. I hadn't known that I had a large butt and thighs till that very morning. But the more I looked at myself, the more I saw what those guys were seeing.

I could feel the fat cake I had gulped down earlier threatening to come back up. I wasn't sure though what was more repulsive: the fact that men had turned my body into a subject of their conversation, the fact that I had discovered that I didn't like what the world was seeing when it looked at me, or the fact that everyone continued to ridicule my mother – blatantly.

Right next to me on the ground between the toilet wall and the fence were two rocks that concealed a gap. In that gap I kept my treasures – my journal and my pen. My journal was an old unused hardcover exercise book, nothing fancy.

I had been hiding it from my grandmother because she loathed secrets – the kind that diaries and journals hold. She had told me once that when my mother was younger she had had a secret diary. Of course, my grandmother read it one day, she had told me.

'Your mother has been dragging debauchery into my house for many years now,' my grandmother had shouted. This sounded even harsher in Setswana. My grandmother's voice had been thick and heavy, like the bags beneath her eyes. It had shaken everything – from the walls of our four-room house to every hair on my body. She raised her voice almost daily but still, I failed to get used it.

'I ripped up the pages and made a fire inside one of those

18

old metal dustbins we used to have before diPikitup. She was dragging the devil's writings and thoughts into my house. I burnt all that rubbish. Manyala hela!'

I sat back down on the ground. I wrote about yesterday and today. I wrote about my mother and about my body, and afterwards I felt much better. I shoved the journal back into the gap, put up the rocks, then walked back into the house.

I walked past the bathroom where my grandmother was bent over, washing our clothes in the bathtub. She heard my soft footsteps heading towards the bedroom and without even looking up at me she asked, 'Naledi, exactly what are you doing outside when the dishes have not even been washed? How many times must I tell you that I don't want you standing outside?'

I turned around, heading towards the dirty dishes, when she ordered that I make her tea. I filled the kettle with water and felt my cheeks getting wet – I was crying again.

'Bathong, where's my tea?' my grandmother yelled from the bathroom.

I wiped my face, then set everything up on a tray and placed it on the four-seater kitchen table. I went to the bathroom and informed Mama that her tea awaited her.

One could tell that in her youth my grandmother had been a fair-skinned, tall, slender woman and it was the years that had shortened her slightly and given her a little bit of weight. She moaned about her knees while getting up from the tiled bathroom floor.

In the living room, she stood by the window, her eyes landing on the gathering opposite our house. Mama sipped her tea slowly, 'Moshebeng. Vuilpop e, sies. Do you see what alcohol does, Naledi? You even look like him. No one is dark in this family except you. Le phatla eo, that forehead, nose and everything else, is exactly like his . . . Wabona, this is what Moruti was talking about when he was preaching about generational curses. My mother did not finish school and she worked in the kitchens. I became exactly like my mother. And look at what has happened with *your* mother. She didn't finish school, and worse, she got pregnant by a vuil, vuil drunkard . . .'

I finished washing the dishes after supper and then sat down to watch the omnibus of soapies I had already seen during the week. Through the window I could see Xolani had left, but other young men had joined Clement and Thabiso. Mama and I retreated to the bedroom for our evening prayers.

'Rrago ke mang?' Mama asked.

'Ke Modimo hela,' I responded.

Mama asked me the same question every night, as if to check to see if I still knew that God and God alone was my father.

She had her back towards me and started off the Bible verse: 'Who shall separate us from the love of Christ?'

'Shall tribulation, or distress, or persecution, or famine, or nakedness, or peril, or sword?' I paused, trying to recall the next line.

My grandmother turned to look at me. Her eyes made me even more nervous. I stammered, then tightly shut my eyes.

20

Fear was thumping in my chest.

'As it is written, For thy sake . . .' Mama spoke loudly, stretching each word.

Finally the words came to me: 'we are killed all day long; we are accounted as sheep for the slaughter. Nay, in all these things we are more than conquerors through him that loved us. For I am persuaded, that neither death, nor life, nor angels, nor principalities, nor powers, nor things present, nor things to come, nor height, nor depth, nor any creature, shall be able to separate us from the love of God.'

My grandmother prayed. She prayed that God would protect us at night. She prayed for our neighbours next door, that God would be with them through their difficult time. She prayed that God would help me in school to do well so that she would one day see me pass matric and become a doctor or a lawyer. She prayed for our church, the pastor, his wife and their daughter, Minenhle. She prayed for my mother, that God would help her turn from her wayward ways. She prayed even harder that God would break the curse that was on the women in our family. She prayed for Ntate Sontaha (whom I had never heard of) who was sick in hospital. She prayed for Clement and Thabiso, that God would deliver them from the spirit of alcohol. She prayed for the young people outside who were with them dancing in the night, that they would be delivered from sin. And after the very long prayer, we finally said, 'Amen'.

We lay in bed facing different directions, still listening to the noise from outside. Just as I was about to shut my eyes,

Mama asked again, 'Naledi, where is your mother?'

She wasn't expecting an answer. But I still responded.

'I don't know where she is, Mama.'

'You know, when you were born your mother didn't know what to name you, and so I said to her that she must call you Dikeledi because you came with tears and conflict. And you wouldn't stop crying. You were just crying and crying and crying. Leina le reng Naledi was suggested by the nurse. So your mother decided on that. She said it felt better to give you a name which means star. It's true that our names carry power. When I said that your name is Dikeledi, which means tears, I was not mistaken.'

Mama was quiet for a moment.

'Goodnight,' she said.

Moriri oa mosali ke lesira

A woman's hair is her veil

Reggae or perhaps hip hop, or maybe kwaito. There was a way in which my mother swayed her hips as she walked that made the eyes of every man near her dance to the heavy beat played by her thighs. By the age of twelve I was already aware of the production she put on.

No one could really blame her. She was beautiful. A yellow bone, whose small frame made her appear more like my older sister than the woman who had given birth to me. It surprised a lot of people, more especially the kids at my school, that I, with my dark skin, had a mother who was light-skinned. A very unfortunate thing to befall me, according to them, to inherit the cocoa-brown skin of Xolani rather than my mother's bright hue. Perhaps this would explain why even Xolani called me 'mnyamane', the nickname given to the darkest child in most black families or the darkest kid in most ghettos. Not once did Xolani ever call me by my name, Naledi.

We had parents' meetings once every quarter and on those four days of the year, with my mother beside me, I received attention from everyone. And then I would go unnoticed for the rest of the school year. That didn't bother me because I was shy. I never spoke if I could help it, not even when pressed to pee while sitting in class. I would sit silently and painfully at my desk, then bolt out of the class when it was break-time to go and relieve myself.

So I wasn't as upset as my grandmother was about the fact that my mother had forgotten about yet another parents' meeting.

'She can't even pick up the phone and call,' Mama ranted as we made our way to my school. 'She has never bothered herself with being a mother. Never!'

All heads turned as we walked into the classroom. Mr Molapo left his class and ran up behind us.

'Le kae, Mme Norah. I see Naledi came with *you* to the parents' meeting today,' Mr Molapo said and smiled.

'Yes, yes, rre, her mother was very busy tonight with work so she couldn't come. But I trust that Naledi has been good?'

I looked up at my grandmother thinking, *What work?*

'Hayi, no, always, you know Naledi – she's top of the class,' Mr Molapo said before rushing back to attend to the parents and pupils he had abandoned.

Adults lied all the time. I was not top of my class – middle maybe, definitely not bottom but certainly not top. And how would Mr Molapo know anyway; he was my grade five teacher two years ago.

To be fair, it wasn't just the male teachers who were mesmerised by my mother's beauty but the little boys too. They

24

would ask, 'Is that really your mother? Yoh, you don't look alike.' The girls in my class were much bolder and would come right out and ask the question, 'Whu, mara why umnyama so, o mama wakho a muhle kanje?' The truth is I didn't know why I was so dark while my mother was so beautiful. My greatest wish was to wake up one day and look like I actually belonged to my family instead of being the strangely dark-skinned daughter of the beautiful yellow bone called Dineo. Dineo, that's my mother's name.

* * *

Back home, my grandmother and I found Dineo stretched out on the sofa watching *Muvhango*, her favourite soapie.

Mama was livid. 'O dutse! You are sitting while I have to be a mother to a child that *you* brought into the world, Dineo!' She looked sternly at Dineo and added, 'You're bringing fleas into my house and I will not stand for it.'

Mama left and I joined my mother on the sofa. During the advertisement break, Dineo asked me what had happened at the meeting, although her interest seemed to be more on other things and not my marks.

'And where was Mr Molapo?'

'He asked about you, and Mama told him that you were busy so you couldn't come.'

'Eish mara, men can't control themselves sometimes tjo,' Dineo said, feigning her dislike of the attention.

When the soapie ended, Mama came back into the living room. She was already dressed in her nightgown and slippers.

'O tsebe ausi, you are going nowhere this weekend,' she said to Dineo. 'My boss is throwing a birthday party for her daughter Anika on Saturday. I will be sleeping over there on Friday to help them prepare, and I will only be back on Sunday.'

'Wait, Mama, so you are leaving on Friday and only coming back on Sunday?'

'Is there a problem, Naledi?' Mama said as she paused to give me *the look*.

'Nnyaa, there's no problem. Le je monate.'

I was being untruthful. There was a *huge* problem. She was leaving me alone for an entire weekend with my mother.

* * *

Friday came and during my walk home with Sindi all I kept thinking about was the weekend ahead.

As soon as I turned into Ndende Street, I could see a car parked in our front yard. I had seen Dineo in that car before on Saturday afternoons; she would either be standing out-side talking to the man inside, or coming out of it with fast food packets and shopping bags. I had never met the owner of the car. It was a very nice-looking car. It was big, black and always shiny.

I stepped into the house and there, lounging on my grand-mother's couch, was a man sipping whiskey with ice cubes in it. He was large, bearded and tucked into an almost too-tight shiny silver suit with pointy black church shoes con-cealing his feet. He looked like meat tightly wrapped up in

26

foil. Dineo sat next to him holding a glass of her favourite white wine. She seemed to be suffering from the giggles.

'If you do that, you'll be rewarded,' the man said.

'And what will you give me?' she asked.

'Don't worry, I know the things that my baby needs.'

Dineo tossed her head back and laughed, flicking her long twisted braids, with her hand rubbing the stranger's thigh.

When she noticed me standing in the doorway watching them, she sprang to her feet, adjusting her black minidress. I was relieved because the sight of her red lace panties was really disturbing.

'Bheki, this is my daughter, Naledi. Naledi, o ke Malome Bheki,' Dineo said.

I was forced to do the black customary pleasantries: stretching out my hand to shake his, and smiling.

'Dumela, Malome Bheki.'

'Hayi, wena o kae, my baby?' Bheki asked how I was in Setswana, through a very strong isiXhosa accent.

'I'm well and yourself?'

'Hayi, ndiphilile enkosi, baby girl.'

He pulled my body towards him, giving me a hug and a kiss on my cheek to round off the small talk.

I didn't like being touched or kissed by grown men, whether they were truly my uncles or not, especially the ones whose lips were wet and smelt of whiskey. I wished he'd let go of my hand and stop gazing at me.

I felt my jaw tighten as he began stroking my hair. Why was

he petting me like a dog? *Please stop touching my hair. Please stop touching my hair.* I wanted to scream it, but kept it inside.

'You don't look alike, Dineo. Who does she look like?' Bheki enquired.

'Serious, you think that we don't look alike?'

'Niks tuu, not even a little bit,' Bheki said as he finally let go of me.

'Who knows who she looks like.'

I sat down on the sofa opposite to them. Clearly my mother was drunk. She was light on her feet and her sentences were slurred.

'Sometimes black people can hold you back. How long do they think they will play the card of being disadvantaged? Take me as an example, a boy who grew up eMonti. I came to Joburg and made things happen for myself. What is stopping others from getting out of their shacks?'

She giggled and nodded at this. Bheki had Dineo eating out of the palm of his hand.

'Naledi, you'll be fine, akere?' my mother asked me.

'Yes, I'll be fine, why?'

'Nothing, 'ska wara,' she said, getting up quickly and almost tripping.

'It's that chardonnay I gave you,' Bheki said, laughing at Dineo's two-stepping. 'Andile Mbatha, the CEO of Mbatha Properties, gave me that wine. Of course Andile Mbatha is someone who loves his wines. Mna I don't really drink it; I prefer whiskey,' Bheki explained in English, speaking through his nose.

28

'Well, like you, he's got great taste,' Dineo responded in Setswana. She grabbed both of Bheki's hands and led the way to my grandmother's bedroom.

'Dineo, the truth is that I intentionally associate with people who have taste and who are knowledgeable. If there's one thing I can't handle, it's an ignorant person,' I could hear Bheki boasting in English, long after they had locked the bedroom door.

I watched television on maximum volume to block out the noise from my grandmother's bedroom. Dineo's giggles had turned into moans and Bheki's bragging had turned into heavy grunts. Eventually the noise died down. About ten minutes later, Bheki walked out wearing only briefs and threw himself on the couch next to me.

'What's your name again?' he asked, clicking his fingers.

'Naledi.'

'Ja, mntwana wa Dineo, tsa mong lethela whiskey le ice pha ko kitchen.'

In a deplorable attempt at speaking Setswana while butchering two or three other languages in the process, Bheki ordered me to get him his drink with some ice. I returned from the kitchen with his bottle and an ice tray, and handed it over to him. He poured himself another drink before changing the channel I was watching.

I had never been alone in a room with a man before, let alone a shirtless man wearing only his underwear on my grandmother's couch. He passed out after a few minutes, snoring like a tractor. He still gripped the glass of whiskey in one hand and the remote in the other.

29

I sat there quietly, trying to think of ways I could get that remote. After about ten minutes, his hand began to loosen its grip. That was my chance.

Just as I was about to grab it, I heard a shout: 'Naledi, o dirang?'

'I just want to watch something,' I said.

She walked straight towards me and in that moment I thought she was coming to slap me. She stretched out her hand. I tensed. Dineo swung her hand straight over my head and began nudging and shaking Bheki before helping him up and to the bedroom. I breathed a momentary sigh of relief before realising that that drunk, hairy man was to spend the night between my grandmother's sheets.

The sleeping arrangements in our house were clear: Mama and I shared the bedroom and Dineo slept on the mattress, which she would put on the floor of our living room.

Throughout the night I heard the noise that came from our rowdy streets. Loud music and bottles being broken – it was a Friday night in Zone 2, after all. But I was accustomed to that noise and could sleep through it any day.

What kept me up was the noise that came through the walls of our very own home. Bheki and Dineo were having a little party of their own. I could hear them staggering back and forth to the kitchen to get refills and snacks. I could hear everything that went on in the bedroom, from their drunken conversations to the thrusting and banging on the headboard. All I could do was sink my body into the floor and pull the blankets over me while mouthing the words to Big Nuz's

'Umlilo' which was being blasted through Ndende Street, till I eventually fell asleep.

* * *

Dineo watched her beau drive off the next morning before strutting back into the house, slowly and purposefully, rhythmically shaking her behind.

She made a show of the news she had for me: 'Get dressed, we are going to Sandton City,' she said, doing a little dance before skipping like a girl my age to the bathroom.

Sandton City was in the expensive hub of Johannesburg. We had to take two taxis to get there. We could have easily just walked fifteen minutes to Maponya Mall, but obviously Dineo wanted to make the day special.

Dineo and I spent the day getting our nails done and trying on clothes. She seemed to have more money than usual. She even had money left over for us to go down to Sis' Nozipho's hair salon to undo my bantu knots and get my hair nicely relaxed when we got back.

Walking into the salon, my eyes immediately landed on the Dark and Lovely boxes with Nonhle Thema's face. Sis' Nozipho had placed them on a high shelf for everyone to see. I was so disappointed when I saw Gugu grab the Beautiful Beginnings box and place it next to me. I was even angrier at myself for being afraid to ask for the one that had Nonhle Thema. My hair wasn't that short, but it wasn't growing fast enough to compete with Minenhle's swaying hair.

'Unjani, sisi?' Gugu was Sis' Nozipho's younger sister. Her

31

brilliant white teeth were on display as she smiled at me. My heart dropped when she asked Dineo to come sit in her chair so that she could redo her front braids. I had hoped that Gugu would do my hair and not Sis' Nozipho, who had no concept of TLC. It didn't matter that I sank my head into my neck or tightly shut my eyes, unable to mask my pain and discomfort. Sis' Nozipho's hand never softened, nor did she reduce the heat from the blow dryer. None of my groans moved her, probably because she was too busy talking up a storm and laughing loudly with my mother to even notice. 'That man I married uyangihlanyisa. Month end you won't find him, u-phuma straight emsebenzini uyophuza,' Sis' Nozipho said, pressing the blow dryer too close to my scalp.

'A man is a man, Nozipho, what can you do? At least you know that he loves you.'

'Mara, Dineo, we don't eat love. I can't go to Edgars to pay my account with love. Basically I pay for everything with the money I get from the salon. Yena, his whole salary is for nice time. And this nice time doesn't include me.'

'At least you are complaining about a man that you have. The rest of us are out here praying for husbands.'

'Wena, praying? Oh please, I saw you with your man who drives a Mercedes-Benz this morning.'

Sis' Nozipho must have been the only person on our street who seemed to like my mother. She told Dineo how she wished she had waited a few more years before getting married, until she had studied further and travelled the world instead of settling down just because of a baby. 'And plus I was pregnant, so yena, he just said he's not doing damages, he just wants to pay lobola once and finish.'

'You're very lucky, Nozipho. Very lucky that he wanted to marry you. Being a single mother is not pap en vleis.'

'Lucky?' Sis' Nozipho raised her voice. 'Lucky with what, Dineo? You know people think marriage is a party. Everybody can't wait to get married. I always say, ngenani emendweni and see for yourself. Yey kunzima lapho, Dineo. Marriage is not a joke.'

Finally she was done. Sis' Nozipho loved to say: 'Beauty is painful and expensive, sistas!' And to be fair, as much as I hated the process of relaxing my hair, I loved having a straight, silky and shiny crown.

The lady who was sitting in the chair next to mine got up once her hair had been finely and intricately braided. The woman's eyes looked bigger. Her forehead had a sheen due to the tight pulling of her hair. 'Sleep with a wet doek – it will ease the tightening,' Sis' Nozipho advised.

'No ways, tonight is not a doek night! He needs to see me. Ha, mark the date – nine months from now, you will see the results of this hairdo.' She then strutted out of the salon, swinging her loaded plus-size curves from the left to the right.

'Owza, yes wena ghel!' Sis' Nozipho chuckled proudly, watching the woman leave.

The women in the salon all laughed and high-fived one another.

I was met with the same admiration when Dineo and I got ready to leave. 'Yoh, zikhulile inwele zakho Naledi,' Sis'

33

Nozipho remarked, taking a step back and looking at the back of my hair in awe, as if she weren't the one who had styled it. My hair was thick, black and now almost touching my shoulders. Sis' Nozipho took a comb and began gathering it in the centre. She made a neat phondo before curling the tips of my hair. I smiled as I looked at myself in the mirror. I knew it! Sindi was wrong about my bantu knots eating away my hair; my hairline had never looked better. I wasn't the prettiest girl, but my hair was the best thing about me. I moved my head from side to side, and indeed my phondo moved in the opposite direction. It wasn't just my breasts that were growing. My hair was growing too.

Huma mhiri, ku nghena mamba

*Out goes the puff adder,
in comes the mamba*

Mama couldn't sleep after five, even on a Saturday. She usually gave me until six-thirty before I had to wake up and get busy. The house had to be spotless before midday. Her Saturday ritual started off with her joining MaKarabo outside just after five-thirty to chat about the pains they were experiencing in their bodies, who had died in the last week, church, and the wayward youth in our community. They talked while drawing beautiful patterns with their brooms on the soil that covered their yards.

Mama was on her knees cleaning the floors of the house, but as always her eyes managed to follow my every move-ment, inspecting if I was putting satisfactory elbow grease into polishing the stoep. My arms were sore by the time I stopped and went to take a bath.

In the afternoon, Mama was relaxing in her own special way – polishing her brass ornaments that were displayed on top of the fireplace – when there was a knock at our door. More of a bang than a knock.

When Mama opened the door, she gazed into the eyes of a raging bull.

'I want Dineo, ukhona apha?' she barked in isiXhosa.

'Dineo didn't sleep here last night, but you can leave her a message,' Mama responded.

'It's okay – ndizakulinda.'

The woman couldn't stand still, shuffling her feet about when she spoke. Her chest was rising and dropping with each word. She must have been in her mid-fifties, a mature, light-skinned beauty with dreadlocks gathered into a taut bun on her head. She was shapely, fitting nicely into her black tights, which she'd paired with a long navy caftan and flat brown boots.

Mama took a deep breath. 'If you want to wait for Dineo, that's fine by me, but not in my house.' She slammed the door in the bull's face.

'Mkhuphe – you can't hide her forever. Andithi she wants my life, so she must come out and look me in the eye like a woman!' the woman was shouting from outside.

Mama sat back down by the fireplace and continued with her polishing.

The noise only died down after thirty minutes.

I didn't understand what she wanted with Dineo. Or what she meant by Dineo 'wanting her life'.

* * *

Dinner was ready. I sat down with Mama in the kitchen, glanced at my plate and almost felt full just by looking at it. It was cabbage and a mountain of pap. There was more pap than cabbage. While Mama was praying over the food, in my heart I was asking God to please improve our meals. We had pap *every day.*

Sometimes it was the hard pap like tonight and other times Mama would make it super soft. And then we had putu days. Mama also loved to make the traditional Tswana ting, and of course every morning we had soft porridge, most times brown and at month's end, white, with a spoon of peanut butter and sugar. I didn't mind the white porridge; in fact, I quite liked it. But heaven have mercy on this black child's stomach, I was completely over pap.

'Amen,' Mama said passionately.

She dug into her meal, taking mouthfuls as if what she was eating were something made by Mme Dorah Sitole herself.

'Eat, Naledi,' she said.

Before I could stick my hand into the white heap, we heard a commotion outside. Not stopping to think about what Mama would say or think, I bolted to the living room window. All I could see was a crowd of people and could clearly hear their profanities.

My grandmother was a proud woman who saw herself as a person who had more dignity and self-respect than the heathens who lived around her. When fights broke out in our community, Mama stayed out of them.

So Mama carried on eating.

'Get away from there!' she said with steel in her voice.

I returned to my seat at the kitchen table. I began to eat.

'Mo shape, hit her!' the noise flared up again.

A bottle broke. Curse words grew wings and flew through the air. Another bottle broke. A woman screamed. The crowd jeered.

A knot developed in my throat. Something was wrong, and Mama knew it too. I had felt it in the pit of my stomach all day and now it was even worse. I grabbed a small portion of the pap; it felt drier than usual as the mass made its way down my throat.

I didn't understand why we were sitting here with Mama watching me force down stones.

A loud thud interrupted us. Someone had scaled the fence, entering our yard. The noise became louder. Mama ran for the telephone and dialled the police.

'There are people fighting in my yard,' she told the officer on the other end of the call.

A pause.

'I said there are people fighting in my yard,' she repeated.

A pause.

'My daughter is being beaten to death!' she yelled.

I forgot Mama's instruction to stay away from the window and darted towards it. I pulled back the curtain and saw the woman who had been banging on our door earlier standing front and centre of the mess. Only this time, the bull was holding a long black sjambok and was whipping my mother, who was rolling in the dirt.

With every lash, the crowd, led by our neighbour Felicia, barked: 'Hit her, hit her, mo shape!' Felicia had a rough-edged, hard tomboy feel about her. She blended in with the chanting men who encircled Dineo.

Dineo kept yelling 'Leave me alone, leave me!' in Setswana. English became a language as distant as its country of origin for many black people in times such as these. Mama put down the phone and ran outside. I charged behind her.

Our neighbour MaKarabo swung her arms around me, and held me tight.

Mama stood between the woman holding the whip and my mother, who was too weak to attempt to lift her body. The bull continued her fight to get to my mother, but Mama pushed her so hard that she fell to the ground.

Dust plumes sprang up and danced, blurring my vision.

'Voetsek, get out of my yard. All of you, get out!' Mama yelled.

I saw flashing blue lights approaching through the brown air. Sirens were engulfing Ndende Street. The police rushed in and the mass darted out like frightened sheep. They ran in several directions, fleeing the trouble they had fuelled.

My mother and the bull were left in the dirt. The police took them both, driving off at full tilt with them tossed in the back like sacks of oranges.

MaKarabo pulled me into the house and sent me to bed. 'It's late and your mother will come back, wena, just sleep,' she said, watching me change into my pyjamas. She made sure that I was tucked in before leaving. I could still hear Mama lamenting the evening's chaos outside.

How could I sleep? I decided to get out of bed.

Mama walked into the house and found me sitting at the kitchen table. She pulled out a chair and collapsed into it.

I got up and made tea for her, then sat back down. I was too afraid to say anything to her. We sat up for about four hours in silence, staring at the walls.

* * *

My mother walked in looking like she had just wrestled a herd of goats back into the kraal. Only a few of her braids were still knotted into a loose bun, the rest scattered in different directions. Her left cheek was grazed and red, and she had cuts on her legs and arms. Her orange dress was torn and had turned brown from being tossed around in the dirt.

'Should I make you a cup of tea?' I asked her.

She nodded. I was aware of every sound, from her shoes landing on the floor, to the kettle boiling, the crickets outside and the clouds gathering in the sky.

With the kettle off and the tea made, and only the sound of the rain now pouring down, the air rested heavily. Dineo was staring at her cup. Mama's eyes had remained fixed on her from the moment she had walked in.

Dineo took a slurp of tea.

'What are you doing bringing filth into my house?'

I had thought I had wanted someone to interrupt the uncomfortable air, but now I missed the silence. The thunder roared and shook everything in our house.

Dineo still looked down at her tea and said nothing. I wished she would just open her mouth and tell Mama she was sorry.

Mama asked again, 'What are you doing bringing filth into your father's house, Dineo?' She bore the look of someone preparing to bury her child.

Dineo was calm when she responded, 'Mama, I am a woman.'

'Then act like it!' Mama slammed her hand on the table. My body jolted. Dineo never flinched.

'You need to stop talking to me like you're talking to Naledi.'

'You are opening your knees for another woman's husband and you dress this child with that money.'

'Bheki is leaving her.'

'Lebelete!' Mama shouted.

Lightning flashed, briefly brightening the kitchen. And again there was silence.

I wished I had listened to MaKarabo when she had told me to go to bed. Dineo was looking at Mama, tears filling her eyes. Then Dineo broke the news that would bulldoze the walls of what I had come to define as my world.

'Kea nyala, Mama,' she said through her quivering lips.

'Jezebel,' Mama's voice slowly rose, 'you will not grease these walls with your sin. Not this house. Not in the name of the Kwena family. Not in my name!'

Mama began to speak in English. The only time my grand-mother spoke in English was when she was talking to white people or reciting the Bible. Scriptures began to pour out of her mouth like the river which flowed out of Eden: 'For we wrestle not against flesh and blood, but against principalities, against powers, against the rulers of the darkness of this world,

41

against spiritual wickedness in high places. Wherefore take unto you the whole armour of God, that ye may be able to withstand in the evil day, and having done all, to stand. Stand therefore, having your loins girt about with truth, and having on the breastplate of righteousness; and your feet shod with the preparation of the gospel of peace.'

She took a moment before reverting to Setswana: 'Pack all your rubbish and get out. Get out of your father's house!'

Mama walked away and slammed the bedroom door shut behind her. The rain continued to pour outside. Mama prayed loudly for what seemed like hours through what was left of the night. Her desperate and painful conversations with God shot through our thin walls and into the living room.

'I'm tired of this,' Dineo said to me while dabbing her wounds with a cloth. 'Zone 2 . . . Mama . . . I'm tired of it all. Listen to her right now,' Dineo said. 'She's a crazy woman. I've been forced to deal with this madness my whole life. Bheki ke motho o sharp, Naledi. I know it will be an adjustment for all of us, but I promise things are going to be so much better with Bheki.'

Dineo said more to me that night than she had ever said to me my whole life. She went on to promise me what sounded like heaven. It was hard to imagine a heaven where big-bellied hairy men walked around topless wearing only briefs.

* * *

Dineo woke me up at five that morning. My two hours of sleep had flown past as quickly as an eagle catching prey. I was exhausted. She had already started packing our possessions into boxes and suitcases.

Mama emerged from her bedroom and got ready to go to church. I hated waking up on Sunday mornings just about as much as I hated waking up on Saturdays to clean. Didn't God say Sundays were for resting?

There I would be in church next to Mama with my eyes stretched widely, forcing them to stay open. Occasionally my head would spring forwards. I would be sitting praying that Mama didn't see that I had just nodded off, but Mama would be so engrossed in the words that Moruti, our pastor, would be saying that she failed to notice the horrible battle I was in, between God and sleep.

But on that day, Mama left for church alone and said nothing to either me or Dineo. She hardly looked at me and I wondered if she understood that every fibre of my being wanted to stay with her.

Some time after Mama had left, the shiny big black car pulled up outside. People made it no secret that they were staring at Dineo and me as we loaded our lives into Bheki's car. Thabiso and Clement were already sitting under the tree washing down the events of the previous night with early morning beers. Felicia stood against the fence of her grandfather's house by the corner. She was one of those who religiously attended mass. A choir member stood with her hymnal in hand, completely forgetting that she was on her way to church.

MaKarabo and Karabo walked out dressed in pure white

clothes and white headwraps, preparing to set off to the Apostolic Church.

'Naledi, o ko kae Mme Norah?' MaKarabo paused to ask about my grandmother's whereabouts.

'O ko kerekeng,' I explained.

'Jwale, what are you doing with all these boxes and bags?'

Dineo turned around sharply, and dumped a box into the boot of the car. 'Keng ka batho ba mo Zone 2? You're always sticking your noses into other people's affairs. Weren't you on your way to church, MaKarabo?'

'One day life is going to bring you to your knees, my girl,' MaKarabo retorted.

Just then Bheki stepped out of his car and pointed his finger at MaKarabo. 'Heyi wena mama fok off, voetsek!'

Karabo interjected and the argument exploded with Bheki, Dineo, Karabo and MaKarabo all breathing smoke into one another's faces.

Clement approached us, I suppose with the intention of putting out the fire: 'Dineo thatha lekhehla lakho nihambe! Leave us in peace!'

Dineo picked up a brick and tossed it at Clement, missing him by a few centimetres. She charged towards him but Bheki grabbed her. He ordered her to get into the car. I had already squeezed myself onto the backseat that was stacked to the roof with our belongings.

'Tsamaya, go!' Felicia shouted.

Amid the laughter and unkind words, I felt empathy pouring from Karabo and MaKarabo. They waved goodbye to me.

When we turned the corner, we saw Mama walking back from church, clutching her Bible and umbrella in her hands. She looked at us. I tried to raise my hand and wave but the only thing that came up were the tears that ran down my cheeks. The car's wheels spun off.

Ubuhle bendoda zinkomo zayo

A man's beauty is judged by his cattle

'Manje, you don't want to go to the Somalian to get amakip-kip?' Sindi asked me with such an intimidating look in her eyes I was almost too afraid to respond.

'No. I can't, Sindi, I have to still walk to the taxis.'

'Oho hamba ke.' Sindi turned with her arms folded across her chest and flounced away.

I didn't understand why she was acting like I was doing all of this on purpose. Of course I wanted to enjoy a packet of amakipkip, and I would much rather gossip about hair and bras than take that lonely walk down to the taxis back to Kedibone's townhouse.

We were staying at Kedibone's house until Dineo and Bheki got married. Bheki and Dineo were getting married in the month of 'Dezemba', as Kedi pronounced it. Staying with Kedi meant I had to learn how to travel to school and back on a taxi, alone. I was still not used to it. I slid open the door, my eyes scanning the vehicle for a seat, but it was full. Why did this driver even stop for me if there was no space?

'Woza phambili, sisi – there's space here for you,' the driver said impatiently.

My eyes widened. An older man sitting in the front seat jumped out and held the door for me as I hoisted myself up into the taxi. I was sitting in the worst seat – the middle seat right next to the driver. Not only was the backrest loose and unstable, which meant that I stood a very high chance of flying through the windscreen if the taxi driver were to apply his brakes, but this seat also came with the responsibility of having to count money received from all the passengers and then distribute the change. Maths was my worst subject.

'Four,' the woman sitting behind me said, digging her fingers into my shoulder to get my attention. I had not even started counting that money before she dug her fingers into my shoulder again. 'Four,' she repeated, passing me more money.

A second later, someone else nudged my other shoulder, saying, 'Three.'

The money was coming in fast.

'Two and one,' the older man sitting next to me in the front said, passing me the money.

Why didn't people just say three – what was 'two and one' even supposed to mean?

'Can we please have our change – sicela i-change bo,' someone from the back of the taxi yelled.

I could feel my panic rising. I feared saying anything to the mean-looking driver. When I finally sent the change out, it was immediately sent back to me because three rand was missing. The older man sitting next to me shook his head at me. 'O kena

47

sekolo, you are even carrying around a big schoolbag but you can't even count,' he sneered.

Walking into the complex, I vowed never again to sit in the front. I wanted to run away to a quiet place but seeing Kedi's neighbour washing his car in the parking lot with the sound system playing at full blast, I remembered that it was a Friday. Weekends were always busy at Kedi's house. I had thought that people who lived in townhouses lived in quiet, sophisticated environments, but there was no difference between that complex and Ndende Street.

I manoeuvred my way past the laundry that was placed in the middle of the passageway on a washing rack and found Dineo sitting on the L-shaped couch with a comb and towel next to her waiting for me.

I wasn't sure whose hand was worse, Dineo's or Sis' Nozipho's. Sitting on the floor between my mother's legs while she tightly twisted my hair was torturous. Being so far from Sis' Nozipho's salon, Dineo had resorted to doing my hair herself. I could be many things, but the girl with the messy hair was not one of them.

Kedi arrived in her slick navy two-piece uniform, which accentuated her boyish build. Her makeup was also eye-catching, finished with a matte lip, signature razor-cut weave, acrylic nails and long eyelash extensions that fluttered like birds' wings with every word she spoke.

'Tsala, I'm back.' Kedi made the usual pit stop by the fridge to pour Dineo a glass of white wine and to get herself a cold Savanna.

'Tsala, so you know akere the story that Bheki is trying to get that woman out of his house?' Dineo said, twisting my hair. 'Does she not go and physically assault my man when he was trying to throw her out?'

'Eng?' Kedi was hanging on every word.

'He had to literally drag her out. Phela, you know she's not a lightweight. She was punching and kicking him, throwing and breaking things. Hey, tsala, it was bad!'

'So this is her thing, vele of going around beating people up? Basically she's Rambo in a skirt?' Kedi continued. 'And lobola, does he not need to pay that before marrying you?'

'Mang, pay lobola to who?' Dineo jumped up. 'Why must Bheki take out money and give it to a witch who threw her own child out like yesterday's rubbish!'

About an hour into Dineo's rant she was finally done with my knots. Soon after, Kedi's boyfriend, Sol, arrived in his GTI. I knew it was him from the music shaking the kitchen windows and from the *vroom, vroom, vroom* as he parked his car. Sol was stepping on his accelerator, enthralling his friends with his theatrics. Seconds later, the kitchen door was flung wide open and in came the usual suspects, Sol and his friends, holding six-packs and plastic bags filled with meat.

The music was turned up. I retreated to the bedroom, to romanticise about a utopia of my own, far removed from the two-bedroom townhouse I was stuck in.

At around three I could hear the noise dying down. Finally I could go to relieve myself without running into strange men and drunk women moving through the house. I opened the bathroom door. Kedi was standing holding my mother's head over the toilet seat. Kedi rubbed Dineo's back, while Dineo's body jerked before allowing a stream of everything she had consumed to pass through her mouth.

'Naledi, come help me,' Kedi said, attempting to lift a limp Dineo.

I didn't move.

'Naledi, come!' Kedi shouted, struggling to balance Dineo. I took Dineo's other arm, and Kedi and I took Dineo to the bedroom.

Two of Kedi's friends were still there the next morning. They were locked into each other's arms under a blanket on the couch. I collected the empty bottles scattered around the house, swept up the broken glass and mopped the stained floors.

It was Bheki who eventually woke the dead. He came out of the bedroom holding Dineo's hand, and told us all to go outside. A white Porsche Cayenne was parked next to Sol's GTI.

'It's yours,' Bheki said, handing Dineo the keys. The guy who had been passed out on the couch a few minutes earlier ran into the house with an unexpected burst of energy to grab a bottle of champagne. He shook it, popped the cork and drenched us all in liquor.

I knew nobody was going to get on their knees to clean up the mess. I was even more annoyed that he had got it on my clothes. No one else seemed the least bit bothered.

* * *

Where were the people? Where was the cow? Where was i-step? Dineo's wedding was strange, but the venue was beautiful. It was quiet and simple. There was a very strict guest list that included a few of Bheki's pin-suited whiskey-drinking friends. Dineo's friends owned every inch of the dance floor and took full advantage of the unlimited drinks at the bar. I floated around in a knee-high, A-line peach dress – the most expensive dress I had ever worn – fulfilling my duties as my mother's bridesmaid.

Kedi was the maid of honour, a title that did not keep her from being her usual loudmouthed, drink-always-in-hand self. Her speech to the bride and groom went something like: 'Ke lenyalo la Dineo today, and she looks stunning. Look who's laughing today. Today you are Mrs Kumbaca to the ones who called you straatmeid. Laugh at them, my friend, because today you are sitting next to your king who was made for you by God.'

Kedi raised her finger high in the air and waved it. 'Halala tsala,' she ululated and was joined by others in chorus.

Se mo tshwere tshwere senatla
Se mo tshwere tshwere senatla
Se mo tshwere tshwere senatla
Ngwana o tshwere ke senatla.

In that moment I became nostalgic. I was transported back to Zone 2, Pimville, Ndende Street. The lavish invite-only wedding must have been Dineo's way of rubbing her success in the faces of all those who had spoken ill of her. Bheki had money and he made no secret of that. To Dineo and a host of others, this meant that Dineo had found herself quite the catch. Never mind his plump frame, broad nose, rough skin and his love of shiny suits – none of that mattered, for as the old saying went: 'ubuhle bendoda zinkomo zayo'.

La go hlabela o le orele, gobane ka moso le hlabela bangwe

If it shines for you, enjoy it, because in future it will shine for others

After the first few weeks of Dineo trying to get me settled into my new high school, still in my old neighbourhood of Pimville, Bheki whisked Dineo off overseas. I was shipped back, alone in a taxi, to Mama's house.

MaKarabo's husband, Ntate Moloi, had a Sunday ritual of sitting out on a camp chair on the small patch of lawn in his front yard, reading a stack of newspapers and listening to The Romantic Repertoire on the radio, the poetic music played by the smooth-sounding Eddie Zondi.

I knew about their Sunday meals from Karabo – she cooked these with her mother and her daughter, Nthabi. They ate two types of meat: chicken and lamb stew with coleslaw, morogo and ledombolo. My mouth would often salivate at her description of the food. She would pass chicken to me across the fence and I'd gulp it down before Mama caught us.

I had once received a beating with a long slim stick from Mama when I had arrived home with a plate of food dished out to me by Karabo.

'Go and pick out a stick from the tree and bring it here!' Mama had ordered. Over time I learned that the thinnest sticks were sometimes not the best option, for their agility caused them to bounce off your skin much faster, giving maximum punishment.

I had eaten the meal from Karabo, churning it down with tears streaming and Mama giving me a malevolent look every time she walked through the kitchen. Ever since, I'd lied to Karabo that I had already eaten whenever she offered to dish up a full plate for me. But still, I couldn't resist a bite of kgogo ya Sesotho cooked by MaKarabo. It struck the perfect balance of tough but tender without the overdressing of spices.

Today, even though I could hear Dave Koz and BeBe Winans's 'The Dance' streaming through Ntate Moloi's sound system, he wasn't sitting at his usual Sunday spot outside. But Thabiso and Clement were chilling under the shade of the tree, watching me as I struggled to carry my schoolbag and two other weekend bags.

Mama had locked the gate and there was no key in the postbox either. My heart sank. I could no longer avoid the two boys across from me.

'Le kae.' I feigned pleasure at seeing them.

'Sharp, Naledi,' Clement said. 'Magriza o ko church.'

I placed my bags on the ground and sat on top of one. I observed the potholes stretching throughout Ndende Street and the kids who had come out to play chigago.

There were four cars parked outside Sis' Nozipho's hair salon, with a healthy flow of women and girls walking in and

54

out through her gate. There were a few noticeable differences, like the new professional board that had a logo along with *Nozipho's Beauty Palour: Quality Hair and Nails.* Further down the street a few guys stood around a gazebo waiting to get their hair cut and beards trimmed.

* * *

It was almost dark by the time Mama came home from church. She arrived with three other women. She rushed towards me. 'Oh no, Naledi, did Dineo just dump you here!'

Mama's church people came into the house, purely out of curiosity, I thought.

'Bathong Dineo o ko kae?' one was shouting from the living room.

'Hey, Dineo is now married, remember. I don't even know if you call that a marriage where there was not even a cent of lobola paid.'

'Whu mara, you know we take these things lightly but we must pray. There is a very serious attack on this family.'

They went on and on while I busied myself with the customary cup of tea for Mama and the visitors. My grandmother was also rambling on about Dineo, leaving me to wonder why old people were so obsessed with tea, and why it seemed to taste even better to them over gossip – the same way that, I'd learned, whiskey seemed to taste better over politics and beer over sports to some people. Their voices rose with their passion.

Mama had kept Dineo and my shelves in the cupboard

empty, as if she knew I would return someday. I took my clothes out of my bags and neatly folded them, placing them where they rightfully belonged. I breathed in the fragrance of my grandmother that slept on her garments and filled the room. It felt good to be home.

I stretched out on the bed. I could hear the women, whose chatter had turned into loud prayers. The bedroom door swung open and two of the women rushed in. One of the women paced about, praying in tongues, while the other one walked straight up to me and placed her hands on my head. Mama and the third lady walked in, with Mama repeating, 'Yes! Yes! Amen! Amen! Oh, yes!'

The hands on me tightened around my head as Mama's friend shook me, rolling her tongue so fast I failed to catch her words. The third lady kept hitting her hand against her Bible, bouncing on her feet. And then like a unified body feeling one another's energy, they all slowly decelerated back to normal again. There was a resounding 'amen' at the end of it all.

After they had left, Mama gave me a bowl of homemade soup with bones.

'Did your mother really get married?' Mama asked.

I nodded.

'Has your mother been sending you to your new school?'

'Yes, Mama, she's been dropping me off and fetching me there every day.'

Mama's eyes widened.

'Bheki bought her a car,' I explained, seeing that she was trying to digest the information I was telling her.

It took her a moment and then she asked, 'Do you know how to get there on your own from here?'

I nodded.

* * *

Things were a little different at my new school. I didn't slip by unnoticed, like I had at my primary school. Dineo's new white Porsche Cayenne had caught the attention of many kids. There was a crowd of about eight boys who would stand by the school gate and await my arrival each morning. They did this to drool not only over the car but over my mother, too.

'Cava lama rim mfana.'

'Double exhaust, yah le iyahamba.'

'Yoh mara le cherrie iyashisa.'

'Yellow bone baba.'

On that morning their smiles quickly vanished when they saw me turning the corner on two legs and not in a Porsche with my hot yellow bone of a mother.

'Eh, and then?' One boy raised his hands to his head. Their eyes followed me as I walked in, a grin on my face.

Sindi was nowhere to be found. She usually arrived first and then waited for me. The school bell rang, and we went to assembly, where we sang 'Tlo moya o halalelang', a hymn that was led by the school's choir, before we recited the Lord's Prayer in both Sesotho and isiZulu.

The head boy read a speech, and then we sang the school song. Three teachers and the deputy principal, with a sjambok in hand, walked between the lines inspecting our uniforms. Sindi was still nowhere in sight.

There was more discipline here, probably because high-school kids needed a firmer hand. They clearly hadn't got the news that teachers weren't allowed to beat kids because just last week I had seen one of the teachers slap a grade eleven boy across the face. Apparently the boy had said 'voetsek' to the teacher when he had told him to get out of his class for being disruptive. Something as small as being late here meant serious trouble.

Sindi eventually walked in at nine o'clock during geography with a late slip in her hand. Her entire face was covered in spots of white cream.

One boy remarked, 'Tjo, manje?', before laughter broke out in the class. Ma'am reprimanded everyone, but this failed to stop the whispers that travelled throughout the room for the rest of the period.

'What's on her face?'

'Maybe they ran out of Vaseline at home so she had to use toothpaste.'

'She's already ugly and now she's made herself worse.'

'How do people come to school with strange diseases knowing that they'll spread it to us?'

Sindi and I had found a new spot where we sat every break. There was a weird air between us. I felt bad for what had happened in class earlier and didn't want to upset her by bringing it up again.

'So I walked to school today,' I said, attempting to dissolve the uneasiness, but Sindi continued to bite into her peanut-butter-and-jam sandwich like I hadn't said a word.

'I'm not worried about getting chickenpox because I've already had it,' I said finally.

'Nawe, Naledi, hao, it's not chickenpox. They're pimples, okay, just pimples!'

I was well aware of the few pimples that Sindi had here and there, but now there were so many. It seemed strange.

'So the cream, is it for the pimples?' I asked, treading carefully.

'Ugogo gave uMa a list of ingredients to mix to make a cream for me at home because she said that those creams that the doctors gave me don't work. Ugogo says that our skins are different from white people's skins so these doctors don't know what works for us.'

'But don't doctors study all kinds of skins, even *our* kind of skin, which is how they know what to give us?'

'Have you ever had pimples, Naledi?'

'No.'

'Have you ever been to a doctor and got a cream for your face?'

'No.'

'Manje?'

When Sindi said 'manje', it simply meant, 'So shut up, because you don't know what you're talking about', in not so many words. I did exactly that.

We were still there, neither of us talking to the other, when Desmond, Thapelo, Siyabonga and Sihle walked by, all with their hands tucked into their pockets. They were the popular boys in grade eight, more for their mischief than their stellar looks, except for Sihle. Sihle was beautiful, like his name. Desmond was the ringleader because he had failed a few times and was older. Thapelo was the prankster and Siyabonga was the one boy who would do anything to be a part of the crew, even if it meant taking the fall.

'Uthini, Ledi,' Sihle said to me as the rest of the group bobbed their heads to say what's up and continued walking.

I waved and smiled. He smiled back and walked away. I had no idea what that meant or why Sihle had been greeting me the last two weeks. Sindi had a mischievous grin on her face.

'I think he likes you,' she whispered.

'Oh please, Sindi, Sihle likes everyone and anyway, I'm not into boys,' I responded.

'Muhle yena,' Sindi said, packing away her lunchbox into her bag.

Sindi and I had never had any conversations about boys, but I understood what she meant about Sihle being cute. He had big brown eyes, caramel-coloured skin and quite a lot of swag for a fourteen-year-old boy.

High school, I was learning, was completely different from primary school. Cute boys like Sihle made my name sound cool by calling me 'Ledi' and they even said 'Hi' to me whenever they saw me. Perhaps I'd been upgraded because they viewed me as the rich kid. I didn't mind the attention at all.

Back home, I called for Karabo, shouting her name across

the fence. She walked out wearing slippers and a thick grey jersey with a small blanket wrapped around her waist – the same way that Mama often wore hers. But it wasn't cold. We were in the middle of summer and the sun was ripping through our blue skies. Karabo appeared gaunt, her eyes ringed with dark circles.

'Sihle, the cutest boy at school, said hi to me today,' I told Karabo.

Karabo confirmed my suspicions of the reasons behind my popularity but in the same breath said, 'Be careful of boys, Naledi.'

Again I told Karabo, 'I'm not into boys. I'm just curious to know why Sihle is suddenly giving me attention.'

I was being untruthful. The attention excited me. I kept thinking about Sihle – did he like me? Did he find me as cute as I found him? It was all so confusing.

Lolo, Karabo's younger brother, arrived back from school in his soccer kit and just like everybody else he was surprised to see me.

'I thought you went to go live with that old man that's hitting things up with your mother?' he said.

Karabo gave him a push on the shoulder, showing him that his comments were inappropriate. But I was never offended by the things Lolo said because I had known him long enough to know that he never meant any harm by the words that rolled off his tongue.

Sis' Nozipho changed her direction when she saw me. She was wearing a brown bodysuit that hugged her curvy body, showing off her flat tummy and accentuating her butt and broad hips. She walked into the yard. 'Dumelang, dumelang,' she almost sang her greeting. Lolo licked his lips and greeted her back, his eyes marking her slowly from her feet to her head. Sis' Nozipho noticed how the sixteen-year-old with raging hormones was looking at her. She smiled at Lolo's wandering eyes. 'Whu, Lolo, shame, you are still learning how to crawl – but you're cute,' she said, caressing Lolo's cheek.

Karabo cleared her throat loudly, and asked Sis' Nozipho what she wanted.

'I saw Naledi and thought maybe I would see my friend uDineo,' she responded.

Her hand was still on Lolo's cheek.

'She's on her honeymoon,' I told her.

'Yoh mara, uDineo is living her life whu shem, uyaphila jealous down,' Sis' Nozipho commented, before walking away.

Karabo and I couldn't help but laugh. Lolo's eyes bounced from one butt cheek to the next, following the rhythm of Sis' Nozipho's buttocks. Karabo slapped him from behind his head. 'That woman is almost thirty. Sies, Lolo!'

'So? Thirty is not old,' Lolo said, walking away.

* * *

'Bath – we are leaving,' was all Mama said, shaking me awake. The sun was not even out yet.

Mama shook her head at me after inspecting me. 'If that's what you are wearing, then make sure you pack a bag with some old clothes you can change into when we get there,' she said.

My grandmother's feet were fast. All the way to the taxis, I jogged to keep up with my bag of clothes strapped on my shoulder. When we reached Bree taxi rank, we got off that taxi and took another one. The sun was beginning to come out and people were filling the streets of Joburg CBD. I still had no idea where we were going.

We took a third taxi before getting out, trekking up a long hill. The streets of that community were nothing like ours. Dogs barked at us from the moment we got off the taxi until we got to the grand golf estate entrance. Mama signed in at the security gate while I tried to collect my breath and my thoughts. There were big houses with security guards driving around in golf carts. I had to remind myself that I was still in Johannesburg and not in the pages of some magazine.

There were even yellow-and-red birds chirping and fluttering around. We didn't see birds like that on Ndende Street. Maybe they were here because there was no loud music coming from anyone's house or open boot to chase them away. There were no kids running through the streets. Nobody was arguing over money or beer. The air smelt fresh.

So this is where Mama worked, I thought, in a massive house that had two kitchens, super-high ceilings and beds covered in pure white linen. It was Mama's hands that washed those linen sheets and made those tiled floors shine. But I couldn't imagine how Mama managed to clean the entire house by herself.

'Come, let's go to my room so you can change out of those clothes,' Mama said.

I couldn't wait to see Mama's room. I imagined a big and spacious room, with large windows that framed the green golf course. Mama led me outside. We walked past a blue pool surrounded by a leafy, sun-filled garden, planted with beds of flowers. Squeezing ourselves into a corner concealed by trees, we reached a short dark passageway that led to a wooden door. That brown wooden door was the entry to my grandmother's room. It was next to a fenced area, with a kennel, where two small dogs who wouldn't stop barking were kept.

It was cold. There was a toilet and shower squeezed into the already tight space. I paused. My mind was wild with questions. Why in this beautiful, massive property would my grandmother's room occupy this unattractive space at the back next to the dogs? Why would they put my grandmother in a room *that* cold and *that* small when there were so many other rooms in the house? Where was the view and the colourful birds? Where was the sun!

A high-pitched voice was shouting from outside.

'Norah, Norah, where are you? I must see you before I leave.'

Mama dropped everything and ran out.

We found a petite, blonde girl dressed in a black tracksuit and black T-shirt waiting in one of the kitchens. She fell into my grandmother's arms.

'Ag, I have rehearsals today,' she said, pulling away from my grandmother.

'No, no, no, you must show me what you have been practising. You have been promising for weeks,' Mama said, shaking her finger in the girl's face.

I was confused about what they were talking about, but more than that, I was confused by Mama's tone. She actually sounded playful.

'Okay, I'll do a short monologue,' the girl said, but was interrupted by an older woman. She had long blonde hair, blue eyes, long legs and was very stylish.

She saw me. 'Who's this, Norah?' she asked, switching on the kettle.

'She's my daughter's child, Naledi,' Mama said. 'She's here to help me wash the windows. Naledi, go and change in my room. The earlier we start, the more we'll get done.'

The playful Mama had disappeared. I retreated to get changed.

Mama walked in with a bucket in her hand. 'Come, Naledi, why are you taking so long? You'll start by cleaning Anika's room. Then we'll do the windows.'

Anika was her name, the blonde girl who had the magical power to make my grandmother playful. Anika had other magical powers, too, she could call my grandmother 'Norah', as if she were talking to someone her age. Anika could sit in the kitchen and talk to Mama while another girl cleaned her big, colourful, messy bedroom. What kind of a girl was this who didn't clean up after herself?

'Wow, Anika!' I could hear Mama clapping. 'Do it again.'

I tiptoed back to the kitchen and peeked in. Mama was standing on top of the kitchen counter washing the window while Anika moved around on the floor in a dramatic way. Sometimes Mama would pause what she was doing and look at Anika with the broadest smile. My grandmother's face literally looked brighter, as if the sun had come in to rest on it. Another one of Anika's tricks.

Cleaning Anika's room took up a lot of time. There were papers and books everywhere. Plays. I had never read a play and had never seen a drama before until that morning in that shiny kitchen. I sat down on Anika's bed and read. I kept telling myself that that was the last page I was going to read, but before I knew it I was stuck. I was stuck on a bed pulled into a world of people I had never met.

'Naledi, how long does it take to clean one room? I need you to help me with the windows!' Mama shouted.

It was impossible to get through all the windows but I didn't think that was Mama's goal because she sounded satisfied with what we had managed to do. I was exhausted by the end of the day. But there was one more thing I needed to do.

I snuck back into Anika's room, took the play, and shoved it in my bag. On my way out, a thought came into my head.

I've already sinned by taking one play. She has so many books, would she really notice if a few more were missing?

'Naledi, where are you?' Mama was yelling again.

I grabbed four more plays and a novel, shoved them in my bag and ran. I did all I could to act like everything was normal as we headed down the steep hill to start our three-taxi commute back home.

That night, I felt like I had a rock resting on my chest. I lay facing up staring at the ceiling, while my grandmother lightly snored. God was watching me. God knew what I had done. Anika the magician had turned me into a thief.

Iqhude yilo elibika ukusa

It is the cock that announces dawn

Bheki's house was dead. Our hallways were filled with silence and so were the brief moments where I found myself alone with him. It had been a year with us living here and I could count the number of things I had said to him on one hand.

I still felt weird about calling this bedroom mine; technically it belonged to one of Bheki's children. But the room saved me from having to look at Bheki's face all the time.

My journal, the plays I had stolen from Anika, and food were the three things that got me through the weekends. I would only leave the room to bath or to get leftover takeaways and snacks from the kitchen.

I had read each play at least a dozen times and knew each character's lines off by heart. They gave me a chance to pretend that I wasn't stuck in a dead house and was instead somewhere else far away speaking with a different accent. I got to be someone else besides this Naledi.

Mondays were the best days. I got to hear Sihle greet me, his dimples piercing into his cheeks. But on that particular

Monday morning, Sihle did more than just say 'Hi, Ledi'. He scooped down, fitting my waist into his arms.

'How are you?' he gazed into my eyes and I felt my heart leap. I had never been held by a boy before.

'Ke sharp.' I flashed a smile as he walked away.

'I told you he likes you,' Sindi whispered.

'No, he doesn't. He was just greeting, hao, Sindiswa.'

Sindi was not convinced.

'There's two of us here but he always only greets you. Is my father's name John Cena? Can he not see me? Worse, he is now even giving you hugs, why?'

At lunch, Sindi and I walked to our usual lunch spot under a large shady tree.

Desmond approached us.

'S'dlala i-spin the bottle – do you two want to play?'

Having a boy like Desmond invite Sindi and me to play spin the bottle immediately confirmed that our status had changed from losers to cool chicks. Of course we were scared. Playing spin the bottle meant that you sat in a circle, spun around a bottle in the centre and whomever the ends of the bottle pointed to had to engage in a lamza, which was a lot more than the peck on the lips that I had seen Thiza give Felicia. The thought of kissing boys had never even crossed our minds and here Desmond stood asking us the biggest question of our lives.

I'm not sure how Sindi and I found ourselves sitting in a group of ten, behind the trees at the back of the school with a bottle that was pointing in my direction. I covered my face with my hands, not wanting to know whom I was to kiss. I didn't even know what I was supposed to do with my tongue once it landed in that person's mouth. I had seen how Karabo and Tau, from *Generations*, would do it, but there was no soft, romantic music playing in the background and flowers sprinkled all over the floor.

'Yoh mfana,' Desmond said. The spectators were running about in a roar of excitement.

I slowly dropped my hands. Siyabonga stood up and moved towards me. I pressed my lips together and shut my eyes. I dreaded the thought of the nose-bleeding Siyabonga engaging in a tongue-rolling act with me.

Sindi and I referred to Siyabonga as 'nose-bleeding Siyabonga' because his nose would always start to bleed at the most awkward times, especially during class. How I wished that it would be one of those times.

He grabbed both my shoulders. 'Vula umlomo phela,' he said, ordering me to open my mouth.

I began to soften my lips, giving a slight opening for him. Without any warning his lips swallowed my lips whole. His head roughly moved from side to side. His tongue swirled about, round and round like a vacuum cleaner. There was loud applause as the nose-bleeding Siyabonga finished with me. I stood there with my lips dripping with his saliva.

'Thatha,' Sindi said to me, passing me some tissues to wipe my wet lips. 'How was it?' she asked. 'It looked scary. It didn't look nice at all.'

'It was worse than it looked, Sindi. I think I'm going to

have nightmares about it for another two weeks at least. It was disgusting.'

'Worse than Bheki's stomach?'

'I would rather look at that beast walk around in his underwear for the rest of my life than kiss a boy ever again.'

'Nawe, Naledi, why did you do it? Mina, I was going to refuse.'

I didn't admit this to Sindi but I knew that I had done it for Sihle. I had hoped it would be him that I would get to kiss. Now the one place where I had found solace was going to be my daily nightmare.

All Karabo could do was laugh herself silly. I didn't get why she was finding this funny. In the midst of our phone call, Bheki's voice went shooting through the walls of the house – he was using heavy isiXhosa which was strange because he always spoke English to Dineo. I couldn't make out Dineo's words but her intonation was trembling.

Bheki's voice thickened. It was continuous, towering over what sounded like stumping elephants. I pulled the duvet cover over my head.

'How's Nthabi?' I asked Karabo.

'She's as naughty as ever. Hayi, mara, her father is so irritating.'

'What did he do now?'

'Absolutely nothing and that's exactly the problem. He does nothing for his child.'

'Well, at least he comes to visit her sometimes.'

'Naledi, what's going to happen when I'm gone? My parents

71

are pensioners with a teenage son, I can't dump the responsibility of my daughter on them.'

'But where would you go? Why would you leave your daughter?'

'Hayi, Naledi, goodnight. You have school tomorrow and Siyabonga to face. Robala.'

Karabo was sick, I had always known that. What was wrong with her? She said it was Nthabi's father who had done this to her. 'The man who dug my grave and put me in a coffin before my time' were her exact words.

I couldn't shake the image of how Karabo looked the last time I had seen her walking around, wrapped in a blanket on a day that was so hot my clothes felt sticky. She had looked old, without a trace of her youthful charm.

* * *

Breakfast was good at Bheki's house. No sour brown porridge in sight. As I ate my Coco Pops, I realised that it was almost seven and Dineo and Bheki had still not come down. I wasn't sure if I should knock on their bedroom door. Finally I heard someone coming down the stairs. It was Bheki. He looked at me sitting on the couch with my schoolbag on my back, in my uniform.

'Yintoni?' he barked.

'Nothing's wrong . . .' My heart was pounding in my throat. It wasn't just Bheki's appearance that had made me nickname him 'the beast' – the man had the ability to beat the fear of God into you by uttering just one word.

'Then why are you sitting there looking lost?'

'It's nothing,' I said shaking my head.

'uNomadzedze is still sleeping,' he sneered before walking out of the door in his shiny suit and pointed shoes.

I did not see my mother for the next three days. When Dineo finally emerged, I found her and Bheki sitting quietly at the dining room table with three plates and Nando's spread out in front of them. She looked like Belle, with her long curly weave and fitted gown, sitting across the table from her beast who was adorned in a tux.

'Naledi, don't forget to take out your washing – Francina is coming tomorrow,' Dineo said after about ten minutes of eating in complete silence.

Silent dinners were something I knew a lot about.

'Hayi kunzima madoda. A man is not only eating chips for supper but he has strange women coming in to wash his shirts and to clean his sheets. And yet, he has a wife,' Bheki snickered to himself.

My eyes immediately darted from Bheki to Dineo. Dineo kept eating.

'Two girls live here. Two. But we must ask another woman to leave her house and her husband to come mop our floors.'

Dineo continued to eat. Bheki's tongue was unchained.

'Umfazi ozithandayo Dineo, cleans, does the washing and cooks for her husband. Yini vele umsebenzi wakho? You don't work, you don't clean, you cook when you feel like it. Why exactly did I marry you, because the only thing you are good at I was already getting before I made you a wife?'

73

Dineo raised her eyes. I had seen that look before. It was the same look she had had that night she had defied Mama. It was the exact same look she had had before she had picked up a brick and tossed it at Clement. I wanted to leave so badly but now was not the time to make any sudden movements.

'Please just remind me, Kumbaca, when you're sitting here handing me a scroll of the things a wife should do, did you ever do the things that you were meant to do as a man? What lobola did you pay, for you to think that you can demand that I should wash your shirts and cook you dinner? Is my inadequacy as a woman not a reflection of your impotence as a man?'

The beast lunged towards Dineo. I shuddered in my chair. Dineo didn't flinch. I could see that Dineo's being unshaken left Bheki defeated. He sucked his teeth, muttering, 'Nxa, Nomadzedze,' before storming out.

I dropped my eyes to the floor and broke out in a secret smile. I was proud.

* * *

Mme Francina was going at it with a vacuum cleaner long before I had even opened my eyes.

'Dumela, mme,' I said loudly, still struggling to get my arm into my gown.

'Naledi, o kae ausi?' Mma Francina said, exerting energy into each forwards and backwards movement of her arm. 'Dineo o teng? I didn't want to disturb her if she's still sleeping.'

74

'They came back home pretty late last night,' I said, even though I doubted she could hear me. I went back upstairs to clean my room and to take a shower. When lunch time came around, Dineo was still in her room. I pulled out two beef patties, to fix Mme Francina and myself a meal.

Mme Francina was forbidden to eat anything except for the bread and butter that Dineo put aside for her. Dineo felt no guilt at eating all kinds of foods in front of mme without sharing. That was the second thing that grated my skin about the way Dineo treated Mme Francina. The first was how she called Mme Francina, who was at least thirty years older than her, 'Francina'. I had not forgotten how it felt to hear Mama being called 'Norah' by that girl. Mme Francina was reluctant, but I eventually convinced her to enjoy the burger. I even poured some cooldrink for her.

'Mme, what does "Nomadzedze" mean?' I asked.

'Someone with fleas because they go from this bed to that bed to that bed,' Mme Francina responded.

My jaw dropped. 'Eng? Bheki – that's what he calls Dineo.'

'Whu che, Naledi.' Mme Francina jumped off her chair. 'I've got work to finish and you should stay out of the affairs of older people, do you hear me!' she said.

What had I done? I had merely asked her a question and meant no harm by it.

* * *

When Bheki was around, Dineo would be functional. On the days when Bheki wasn't around, she stayed tucked away, only

75

coming down to get something to eat before heading back to her bedroom. She moved about sluggishly, dragging her feet along the floor.

'You are a girl, Naledi, you must pick up your feet when you walk!' I would hear Mama's voice in my head whenever I saw Dineo doing this.

She never seemed bothered by my look of disapproval. 'You'll just order something to eat if you can't find anything in the fridge akere,' she would say to me instead, sauntering back to her bedroom.

I got along just fine being alone. I watched movies and I would write about the sleeping beauty called my mother and her zombie-like ways in my journal. I spent hours lying on the bed, staring at the ceiling, thinking, before drifting into slumber. That was the plan for my Sunday. With Dineo still curled up in her dungeon, I woke up to make myself a toasted cheese-and-bacon sandwich before throwing myself onto the soft white couch in the living room.

Almost instantly, I felt something shoot from my vaginal area. I got up very slowly, looked down and saw the red stain on Bheki's white couch. I ran to the bathroom and pulled down my panties. Drip drop, and then slowly it streamed down my thigh and onto the mat on the bathroom floor. I panicked, grabbing huge chunks of toilet paper and holding the bundle tightly against my vagina. I swung open the door and ran to the bedroom, placing the folded toilet paper onto the middle section of my fresh purple panties. Once I felt the situation was slightly under control, it was time for a clean-up. After

76

scrubbing hard for a good amount of time, the red stain on Bheki's couch turned back to white. I headed back to the bathroom, and on my knees I scrubbed until the cream mat returned to its normal colour. The next stop would be my mother.

'Dineo. Dineo, I need to tell you something,' I said, knocking on the bedroom door.

Silence.

'Dineo!' I hit harder against the door.

Silence.

'Dineo, I'm bleeding! Dineo, tlhe!'

'Hey maan, Naledi, go away!' she shouted.

For the first time in my life I prayed that Bheki would return the next day. By morning I had gone through three underwear changes, and I had to change my bedsheet and pyjamas.

Bheki strolled in at seven o'clock at night after the longest thirty-two hours of my life. Finally Dineo surfaced.

Umfazi uyabekezela

A wife must be steadfast

'Naledi, has *Muvhango* started?' Dineo came running into the living room with a glass in her hand. 'Make space,' she said, squeezing herself into the corner of the couch where I was sitting.

'Bathong, Dineo, there is plenty of space on the couch – why must you squeeze yourself where I'm sitting?'

'Shh, it's starting,' she said.

Dineo seemed much lighter than usual. This was strange considering the glass she was holding was filled with orange juice and not white wine.

We were watching a vital scene between Ranthumeng and Thandaza, when Bheki staggered in, reeking of cigars and whiskey. He made his way towards us.

'Why must you leave now that I'm here? Sit down and watch your soapie,' Bheki barked when I stood up to leave.

I obeyed and sat back down.

'You can't force her to sit here with you while you are drunk,' Dineo said.

It took Bheki less than three seconds to go from zero to a hundred. I was right to want to leave.

'Sun'qhela, Dineo, do you see who you're talking to!'

I breathed a sigh, preparing myself for yet another one of their showdowns. Bheki began to list all the things he had given Dineo. Dineo had nothing and therefore had no say about anything that happened in that house, he went on.

Dineo countered with the pair now both on their feet in the middle of the living room.

I lowered my head and tried to avoid looking at them.

'Ndizokubetha, Dineo!' Bheki threatened.

Dineo dared him. 'Go ahead, hit me. Do it in front of Naledi so that she can see for herself that not even a circumcised penis and days on a mountain could turn a boy like you into a man.'

Bheki clenched his fist and knocked my mother to the other side of the room. He took off his belt and began thrashing her. She pleaded with him, struggling on the tiled floor, trying to pull herself away. Each time Bheki's belt bounced off Dineo's skin, I shuddered.

He thrashed her till he ran out of breath, his face dripping with sweat. His eyes met mine. Bloodshot red. I was paralysed. I feared him, now more than ever. I could hear the thudding of my heart loudly in my ears.

Bheki passed his belt through the loops on his trousers that hung beneath his oversized belly. He pulled his keys out of his pocket and left. I looked down at my mother who was still curled up on the floor, groaning.

I saw blood beginning to circle her midsection. She held on to her belly tightly and screamed.

'Naledi, call an ambulance,' the words struggled out of her mouth.

It took about twenty minutes before she was rushed off to the hospital with me sitting in the back of the ambulance as she lay on the stretcher still bleeding.

I stood frozen in the middle of the reception area trying to piece together my thoughts. I was alone. I was without Mama, without Karabo, without Sindi, without MaKarabo or even Mme Francina.

After what felt like hours, a nurse ushered me to the ward.

'Woza, your mother is fine,' she said, devoid of any emotion.

I walked into the ward and looked at my mother. She looked nothing like the woman I knew. She looked lifeless. My lips began to move and I muttered the one thing I knew to say even in my sleep.

'As it is written, For thy sake we are killed all day long; we are accounted as sheep for the slaughter. Nay, in all these things we are more than conquerors through him that loved us. For I am persuaded, that neither death, nor life, nor angels, nor principalities, nor powers, nor things present, nor things to come, nor height, nor depth, nor any creature, shall be able to separate us from the love of God.'

After reciting that scripture for years, it finally made sense. In Dineo's almost lifeless body, I could see God keeping her heart pumping.

My grandmother walked in and found me standing by the window. She bent down, turned me around, then back again.

She looked at my arms and legs, before staring at my face.

'Mama, I finally understand what it means,' I whispered to her.

It didn't seem Mama knew what I was talking about. She pulled a chair over to the bed and sat down. She grabbed me and held me tight in her arms. With my head pressed against her chest, I cried about it all. I couldn't remember a time when my grandmother had held me that close. I cried about being forced to leave home. I cried about Dineo's marriage to Bheki. I cried about how much school I had missed. I even cried about that horrible kiss with Siyabonga.

'Naledi, why didn't you tell me that Dineo was pregnant?' Mama asked, pulling me away.

I looked at my grandmother confused.

Mama continued to hold me at arm's length, and stare. She then got up and took me by the arm and moved me towards the bathroom. I looked down at myself and it was only then that I realised that I had been standing wet in my own mess and didn't even know it.

So I had left a stain on Bheki's white couch after all.

NORAH

'Fiela, fiela, fiela ngwanyana'

*Sweep, sweep, sweep girl**

'Wake up, Naledi! A girl must wake up and sweep before the sun is shining.'

Why was Mama waking me up that early and why was she telling me to go sweep? Mama never asked me to sweep.

The cold was brutal, biting into my skin even through my thick, hooded jacket. I was still trying to gather my thoughts when it dawned on me that teaching me how to sweep was Mama's gift to me.

I was sneezing continually, my nose running, failing to cope with the dust that sprang up with each swift swipe. Next door, MaKarabo was sweeping too. She laughed, amused that I couldn't detect where the wind was blowing from; it kept scattering the dirt I was trying to gather.

'You are just like Karabo – lazy. You can't even do something as simple as sweeping. Who are the poor men that are going to marry you young girls of today? You are spoilt because of the rights that Mandela gave you. You come into our houses and you tell us about feminism and independence. There's no word for "feminism" in any African language because those things came with white people and democracy. Look at the divorce rate, all because women want to be men.'

MaKarabo was wrong. Yes, I wasn't great at sweeping but it was also August – the windiest month of the year. Everyone knew how dusty the township was in August. It had nothing to do with Mandela, white people, and feminism. Still, I was grateful that she showed me what to do, even while chastising me and all the other young black girls who didn't wake up at the crack of dawn to clean.

'Naledi, look where the wind is coming from and sweep in the same direction as the wind is moving. I mean this thing is logic. Kante, does this Mandela education only teach you about rights and they neglect to teach you about logic?'

Back inside the house, Mama was sitting at the table, her Bible open in front of her. She began to read to me.

'Who can find a virtuous woman?' Mama always sounded proud and read with such passion when she read the Bible. 'For her price is far above rubies. The heart of her husband doth safely trust in her, so that he shall have no need of spoil. She will do him good and not evil all the days of her life. She seeketh wool, and flax, and worketh willingly with her hands.'

That scripture was my grandmother's second gift to me.

'This is the sort of woman that God wants you to become, Naledi – remember that as you are busy celebrating. Today *you* will make the porridge,' Mama said, closing her Bible and getting up to leave the table.

One could hardly consider this a celebration. I was surprised by Dineo's phone call. Months had passed since I had last spoken to her.

'Happy sweet sixteenth, Naledi. O gole o gole o gogobe.'

'Thank you, Dineo,' I said before hanging up.

I had nothing more to say to her.

* * *

Mama was officially retiring. Already way past sixty, she said she was tired.

On her last day, she asked me to help her to get the rest of her things from Anika's house. So we were back in the small cold room, where we listened to the two dogs barking while we packed away some of Mama's things. We walked into the kitchen and found Anika making tea. She had placed two small cups on saucers on the kitchen island. I didn't know Anika could make tea. It seemed to me like everything was done for her.

'Oh, Nalady, you're also here,' she said, walking towards the cupboard before returning with another cup. Anika added the teabag and boiling water in my cup. She then sat next to Mama and held her hands. 'Oh, Norah, this house is going to feel so empty. I left rehearsals early so I could say goodbye. I don't know where any of us would be without you. All the advice you gave me because some silly boy broke my heart. You really have been like a mother to me.'

That girl's mouth ran like a motor. I looked up to see if my grandmother was annoyed and was instead shocked to see tears falling from my grandmother's eyes. Mama only cried when she spoke to God. The incredible magician was pulling tricks out of a hat. What Mama said next left me floored.

Mama took a sip of tea. 'Oh, Anika! Know that I love you . . . You are an amazing young woman.'

Mama never told me she loved me. Mama couldn't even say happy birthday to me, let alone call me amazing.

Anika handed Mama a photograph of the two of them. Mama looked at it, then held it close to her chest.

Anika had a way of revealing parts of Mama I never knew existed. She had a way of unearthing desires within myself I didn't know I had. I didn't have many photographs of me and my grandmother, but I suddenly wished we had taken photographs together.

'I'm so excited that I finally get to play the lead in a production,' said Anika.

'I still can't forget the first time I saw you acting. You stood in front of so many people and you were not even scared.'

'Oh no, Norah, I was so nervous. I'm always nervous.'

'Then you hide your nerves well, my girl.'

'I just love it,' Anika explained.

'Me too. I also love it.'

Anika and Mama turned to me. Anika had a smile on her face. Mama looked stunned.

'Hao wena, since when?' Mama asked.

I had got so sucked into their conversation that I had let my secret passion spill all over the kitchen table.

'Naledi, since when are you an actress?' Mama repeated.

I understood where her shock was coming from – nothing

85

about me spelled movie star. I had always been shy. I'd been exploring the world of stories secretly for so many years but something about that world made me feel like I belonged.

'Sweetie, if you love it, do it,' Anika said. It was that simple to her. 'And you speak so well, I'm sure you'll make it,' she added.

I'm not sure why Anika thought that was a compliment. I doubted that she would have said that to a white kid.

'What do you mean?' I asked.

'Hmm?'

'Is it a strange thing that someone like me can talk?'

Anika's eyes opened wider. 'No, no, I mean, of course someone like you can speak. What I meant was, you know like—'

'Hayi maan, Naledi, what's wrong with you,' Mama cut in. 'Anika is helping you, so listen and stop asking questions that have no direction.'

I wished that Mama would have let Anika finish explaining. I was hoping to hear her answer. Instead, Anika and I talked about what I needed to do to prepare to study drama.

'And I have a whole lot of scripts and things I can give you. If you need help, I'm just an afternoon cup of tea away. Oh, and a taxi ride away,' she said.

'It took three taxis to get here,' I corrected her.

'Jesus Christ, three taxis!'

I was almost excited to see Mama shut down Anika for being blasphemous, but Mama said nothing. She didn't even flinch.

Anika giggled. 'So I'm just a cup of tea and *three* taxi rides away. And we all know how entertaining those taxi rides are.'

86

Anika did not look like she had seen what a taxi rank looked like on TV, never mind ever having been in a taxi.

'So you've been in a taxi?' I asked.

'Huh?'

'You've been in a taxi, right?'

'Oh, no! But Norah tells me all about her adventures,' she said.

God bless her ignorance, I thought. She didn't have a clue about what our lives were like. Hearing stories and living the story were completely different. But Anika was sweet. Very sweet and kind.

She seemed not to pick up that I found her irritating, though. 'Here you go, Nalady,' she said, giving me a pile of scripts and novels and even poetry books.

I wanted to correct her – *My name is not Naa-lady* – but she had given me all that stuff. I didn't have to steal them like I had planned.

'Are you not going to say thank you?' Mama gave me a nasty look.

'Thank you, Ah-nih-kah,' I said, ensuring that she heard that I had made a conscious effort to pronounce her name correctly.

I left that afternoon carrying a whole lot of literature and even more unanswered questions.

When MaKarabo came over later, I couldn't hide my excitement about becoming an actress one day. In a strange way, speaking to Anika about the future had lifted my spirits. I felt alive again. MaKarabo was thoroughly impressed that I had set my sights on going to university for acting.

'Good for you, wena Naledi. Kore very soon we will also be seeing you ko *Generations*?'

It seemed that *Generations* was *the* pinnacle for an actor, according to the black people around here. Saying that you wanted to become an actor automatically meant that you wanted to perform alongside Connie Ferguson.

I politely laughed, reserving my comments. I was not one to crush anyone's fragile dreams.

Lebitla la mosadi ke bogadi

A woman's grave is at her husband's home

'It's painful when you are an orphan, the world treats you like an unwanted disease,' Mama said as we were packing our clothes into our big weekend bag.

Mama's mother had died in some kind of fire when Mama was young. She had no siblings and the only family Mama ever made mention of, and then only rarely, was my grandfather's family, the Kwenas.

As we left the house, she stopped. She began to pray. 'Rra Rra, we are going into a household that is ruled by darkness, but let us become the light. Even the evil spirits that are working in the hearts of those people, we know by your name that they will fail. No weapon formed against us will prosper. Amen.'

I had never travelled so far before in a taxi with Mama. Our journey that day was to Bloemfontein for a ceremonial laying of a tombstone for my grandfather, who had died thirty-four years before. This was both my grandparents' place of birth.

When we arrived, Mama led me straight up to the small house that was built in the middle of a huge yard. I couldn't

89

imagine having to sweep that entire yard. The front door was open, with men walking around in blue overalls, the women in aprons and doeks.

'Bathong, ga se Naledi o? My goodness, but you have become so fat!'

'Who does she take after? She doesn't look like us.'

'Ebile, she is dark. This is the first time I see a child this dark in the Kwena family.'

I was moved around the house, shown to different women as if I were some rare jewel that was picked up on our way there from the Big Hole. They hugged me and kissed me, smiled at me, all the while throwing what sounded like insults at me.

Was I really that fat? But those were the words I heard all weekend long even from other fat women. Instead of someone saying, 'Hello, how are you?', they greeted me with, 'Oh my goodness, what are they feeding you in Gauteng!'

Mama seemed distant. It was almost like she wasn't part of the family. My grandfather had two sisters who never seemed to run out of ill words to say about my grandmother. I felt compelled to go to stand with her, left outside chopping onions while the rest of the women stood in the kitchen chatting and drinking tea. There was already a tub full of onions. I didn't know how Mama could chop onions so fast and without any tears. I chopped too, looked up to the sky, tried to blink away the tears, and failed. They came pouring down my face. I sniffed and sniffed because my nose became runny, wiped my tears with my apron, and continued to chop.

There were five sheep bleating just around the corner, where most of the men were. The bleating was a clear indication of what was taking place there, which prompted Mama to say a quiet prayer. When Mama finished praying, she said to me sternly, 'Don't you dare eat any of that meat. These people are slaughtering and spilling blood for ancestors. We know and follow one God. We do not participate in the worship of any other gods.'

I looked up and blinked, then turned to my grandmother, and said, 'Yes, Mama.' I sniffed and continued to chop.

The noise levels increased from the women in the kitchen as the night grew darker, and I became suspicious of what was actually in those mugs. I knew all too well what drunkenness sounded like. My grandfather's sisters spoke the loudest, their words slipping carelessly off their tongues – they slurred and cackled.

'Kore, Norah, when last did she come here? I even forgot that you had a ngwetsi in this house,' one woman asked.

Mama shook her head and chopped more vigorously.

'Of course she would be afraid to show her face here, knowing very well that she took my brother and had him killed!' one of my grandfather's sisters said.

I looked at my grandmother. She looked up at the stars above us and started blinking.

*   *   *

By three the next morning, Mama and I had finished chopping the onions and preparing the samp and ting ya mabele. One of the relatives had opened his car so that Mama and I could sleep in it. Mama was in the passenger seat and I was stretched out across the backseat with a blanket over me. We were given only one blanket to share. Mama said she wasn't cold, that I could have the blanket to myself and fold it in two to make it thicker. I didn't understand how she didn't feel cold because that place was beyond freezing. It never got cold like that in Joburg.

The cold – or the millions of questions I had in my mind – made it difficult for me to fall asleep. I could feel that Mama was still awake too. I had never asked any questions about my grandfather because I knew better. But at that point, even with my heart pounding in my chest, I had to get a few answers.

'Mama, what happened to ntatemogolo?' I said slowly, sitting up in the backseat.

Surprisingly, Mama didn't shout at me but opened up instead.

She described my grandfather as a tall, fair-skinned and very handsome man. They had met here in Bloemfontein.

'He was very naughty, that one. There I was carrying bread from the spaza shop and this man asked to walk me one day. He offered to hold my bread and I told him, "No, thanks, bread is not heavy, I'm sure I can manage." I was showing him that if he wanted me he would have to prove himself to me first. Women were not easy back then, not like now where you just open your knees for the first boy who pays you a compliment.'

In the dark I blushed at the indirect mention of sex but I

was enthralled by Mama's storytelling. My grandmother's words, in our native language, sounded poetic and beautiful as they poured out of her.

She continued: 'A man worked for the affections of a woman because it was in the chase where he proved to her that he was after her heart and not her body. Your grandfather studied my patterns and knew where I would be and at what time, just so that he could romance me with endless stories about our future.

'"Five children or maybe six," he said, "that's how many we will have. We will live on a big piece of land where we will raise them. You'll be doing the cooking and cleaning and I'll be doing the hard work."

"Haa," I told him, "do you think that cooking and cleaning every day is not hard work, especially for a husband and six children?"

"Oh, so you do want me to marry you?"

"I never said that!"

"You just said that I will be your husband and you will have my six children!"'

Mama laughed as she related this silly story to me. It was like I was seeing my grandmother for the first time. This young light-hearted woman she described was nothing like Mama.

One day, they had journeyed together by train to the city where gold was buried in the soil.

'It was a loooong trip. We had heard that Johannesburg was not only a city where gold lay but a place where waters flowed

93

from taps. But living in Soweto at a time when peace was an ideal that we dreamt of and never touched, it became hard to keep out of the struggle when riots were taking place right at your gate. How could you keep your nose clean when filth had claimed our streets and our dignity?'

Mama said ntatemogolo had started attending meetings and rallies. He joined a prominent political party and very soon he was leading the meetings. Suddenly, Mama sang:

> uMandela uthi ayihlome
> Wena uthi ayihlome
> uMandela uthi ayihlome ihlasele
> Siyaya ngoMkhonto weSizwe eLusaka
> Wena uthi ayihlome . . .

In early 1981, Mama had found out she was pregnant. 'Understand, Naledi that a man does not cry. When I told your grandfather he cried right in my arms. I was over forty when I fell pregnant. It's not an easy thing to be married for so many years and be unable to give your husband a child. Your main job as a woman is to expand and build the home.

I could feel her sadness consuming the space between us.

'To this family, I was the woman who had taken their son away to Johannesburg, got him involved in politics, and I couldn't even carry a child. They told your grandfather to take another wife, but he loved me too much. He told me that he could never bring himself to hurt me in that way.'

Mama had felt that finally everything would be okay. My

94

grandfather had been arrested several times but now that she was going to have a baby, he had made a promise to her that he would put politics to bed.

'One day he left for work in the morning. He kissed me goodbye. And that would be the last time he would do so. He was found beaten and stabbed to death in the bushes.'

Mama's voice was shaking, rising as she told me this.

'Eight days, Naledi! Eight days without sleeping and struggling to even lift a spoon to put food in my mouth. How could I sleep when I didn't know if he even had a blanket where he was? How could I eat when he could be starving in the streets somewhere? Eight days!'

I felt helpless. I didn't know whether to place my hand on her bent back and soothe her or even offer her a tissue. Gone was the bull that kept the walls of our house standing. She had never appeared this broken before. I did nothing, and after a while she looked up at me.

'One day a boy found his body, lying in an open plot. I knew it was *them* that had killed him. They never bothered to investigate what happened to him. Just like that, they took him from me. Your mother was born early because I was so devastated. She was my gift to him – that's why I named her Dineo – but he never even got to hold her.'

I knew that Mama was a hard woman with a sharp tongue, but I realised then that, once upon a time, Mama had been soft and giddy like any other girl. Mama wasn't born hard – she *became* hard.

Intandane enhle ikhothwa ngunina

*A good orphan is licked
by his mother*

Mama once said to me that the day you stop doing things for yourself is the day you start to die. I stared at her lying ill on her bed. Was she getting sick because she had retired? But Mama had cleaned another woman's house for a living and now spent her days cleaning her own house even more obsessively. Surely that made her feel she was doing something of purpose, not just sitting at home waiting for the hour of her death?

Being sick didn't suit her. She was too strong to be lying helplessly like that day after day. But with each passing day, she became worse. After a week, I placed a bucket by her bedside because she had become too weak to run to the bathroom. Pushed to my limits, I dialled Dineo's number. It went to voicemail. I called again and Bheki picked up.

'Dumela.' I still had enough respect to greet him. 'Can I speak to Dineo?'

'She's busy right now; I'll tell her you called.' He was his usual arrogant self.

'Mama is sick,' I cut in quickly before he could hang up.

I heard him mumble something to someone. Obviously Dineo was right there next to him.

'Bheki, can I please talk to her?' I pleaded.

'How many times must I tell you that she's busy,' he hung up.

Next door, I found MaKarabo sitting watching television with Ntate Moloi and their granddaughter Nthabi. I had not bothered them about this because they had their own load to deal with, what with Karabo's health and all.

'MaKarabo, Mama is not well,' I said.

MaKarabo came rushing to our house to see what was wrong, and then ran back to her house to fetch Ntate Moloi to take my grandmother to hospital. Apparently Mama's sugar was high. I had no idea that my mother suffered from diabetes, hypertension and a list of other things. I also didn't know that there was a strict diet she had to follow. MaKarabo said that most black people were like that and that their sugar went up all the time. Her exact words were 'sugar loves us'.

The doctor explained that diabetes is higher in the black community. 'She has to watch what she eats,' he warned.

Mama spent a week in hospital and I had to stay at Ma-Karabo's house. Unlike most houses around our neighbourhood, they had a couple of extra rooms, including two outside rooms. Lolo occupied one and I, the guest, slept in the other one during my stay.

* * *

97

My first Sunday at the Moloi household was almost everything I had imagined: morogo, kgogo ya Sesotho, coleslaw, ledombolo and lamb. I was chopping the vegetables that Lolo and I had gone to buy earlier. I was helping MaKarabo cook since it seemed Karabo couldn't.

'MaKarabo, what's wrong with Karabo? Did she go to the doctor?'

MaKarabo dropped everything she was holding and looked at me as if I had sworn at her. I wished I could take back my words but it was too late. I wanted to run but my legs were ploughed into the floor.

'Do you always ask such things ngoana oa Dineo? Do you always go around digging into other people's dustbins?'

MaKarabo's response meant two things: mind your own business and I'm not going to tell you a single thing.

After lunch, an unusual silence filled the house. I had become accustomed to Ntate Moloi's Sunday date with his newspaper while playing the radio loud enough for us to listen to it next door. Since Eddie Zondi's passing a few months ago there was no more Romantic Repertoire and Ntate Moloi preferred the radio off than to listen to anyone new. Karabo was in the bedroom sleeping, while Nthabi, Karabo's daughter, played with her dolls, and Lolo and I were on the couch, chatting as usual. Lolo was three years older than me. I found him very funny, always filling my ear with horror stories and gossip from the neighbourhood.

'The girls in our street are too forward – they are always making a noise. Actually, the girls around Zone 2 generally are too much. That's why I prefer older women, wabona,' Lolo said.

'Older women like who?' I fished.

'Type yaka is someone with a big bum and a small figure with nice perky breasts,' Lolo explained, using his hands to paint the image.

'Someone like Sis' Nozipho?' I said, knowing that Lolo's eyes often danced around her curves when she walked by.

'Mxm waphapha,' Lolo said, failing to hide his grin.

My conversation with Lolo was entertaining but I couldn't help sneaking towards Karabo's bedroom when no one was looking. With only my head peeking through the door, I whispered, 'Karabo. Karabo, it's me, Naledi.' She opened her eyes and smiled.

* * *

I found Karabo sitting on the couch after school the next day. Luckily I had bought an extra packet of amakipkip, which I offered her. Karabo struggled to swallow the first handful of colourful township-styled popcorn before completely abandoning it, leaving me to munch two packets on my own. I didn't mind, though.

'Where . . . is . . . that . . . boy . . . what's . . . his . . . name?' she asked, straining to get an entire sentence out of her mouth.

'Yoh, Karabo, you still remember Sihle,' I said, blushing.

'Oh, yes, Si-hle,' Karabo drawled. 'Kana, what happened . . . with . . . the two of you?'

'Nothing. Absolutely nothing.'

99

'But you've liked this boy since grade eight, Naledi, and you've done nothing about it all these years?'

'I don't think I've ever really been his type. But yoh, he's getting cuter by the day,' I said, gushing.

After that, I hardly saw her again during my stay. I knew she was in her room most of the time. To make up for it, I spent long days outside playing diketo with Nthabi, just like Karabo had done with me when I was little. I had missed her more than I realised.

Dineo showed up two weeks after Mama's return. She found me sitting outside on the stoep writing in my journal. She looked good and smelt even better.

'Naledi, how are you? Where's Mama?' she asked.

I kept my eyes on her as I spoke. 'Mama is inside sleeping.'

'Mama sleeping? During the day? On a Saturday? That's very strange. Are you sure she's sleeping?'

I made a point of repeating her words back at her. Maybe she'd hear me then: 'Yes, Dineo, Mama is sleeping, during the day, on a Saturday.'

Inside, Dineo headed straight for the fridge. It held only a jug of cold water and some butter.

'Is there nothing to eat? I'm so hungry. Did Mama not cook?'

Maybe Dineo was sick, I thought. That would be the only reasonable explanation for her behaviour. It had been months since she had been to my grandmother's house and weeks since she had called to check in, and now she walked in like everything was okay.

'Like I said on the phone the day I called you, Mama has been sick.'

She paused and looked at me with that *I have no idea what you are on about* face. 'Naledi, you know I always deposit money into Mama's account, so don't act like I have abandoned you,' she said.

'Mama hasn't been well. How is she supposed to go to the bank? Mama is busy dying and you can't even pick up the phone!' I had never raised my voice at anyone before, let alone my own mother.

'Askies, Naledi, Bheki took my phone so I couldn't make calls. I heard you call the other day but he refused to let me talk to you. He just gave me back my car and that's why I came.'

Dineo's phone rang. She spoke for a minute to the person on the other end and then she said, 'Okay, I'm coming now,' before hanging up.

'Naledi, I'm leaving five hundred rand. It's all I have in my purse right now. Make sure you go to Nozipho to relax and twist your hair. You can't walk around with a head that looks like that; it's a mess. I'll deposit money straight into Nozipho's account. I have to go.'

I watched her get into her Porsche and drive off.

I grabbed the money and a few empty plastic bags, and took a walk down to Maponya Mall to buy chicken pieces and vegetables.

Five hundred rand, and five minutes. After months, that was all.

* * *

101

On my way back, I heard a voice behind me: 'Hao, Mnyamane, you're still alive?'

Xolani.

'Ngibone uMa wakho. Ja neh, she's now an upper-class woman who drives a Porsche, she doesn't see us nobodies any more. But let me tell you something. Nothing is for free.'

He was drunk as usual.

'Ja mara, women are so cheap and dumb, they sell their souls for a car and house that's not even in their name.'

I tried to walk a little faster, ignoring the heavy plastic bags that were cutting into my fingers, but he stayed close behind me, still speaking at the top of his voice.

'You must know that Dineo is paying a heavy price for all those things. It's called a contract. In a contract there are terms and conditions. I buy you a Porsche; you must give me something in return . . .'

Finally I reached home and would not have to listen to that man any more. Still, he continued to shout as I struggled to open the gate: 'Mnyamane, you say I'm your father, so why are you ignoring me? Mnyamane!'

Clement was sitting at his usual spot under the tree. 'Hey, ndoda, leave Naledi alone,' he said.

'Hey, Clement, don't you have a beer for me?' Xolani asked, staggering in Clement's direction.

I closed the gate and went into the house.

Botlhale ba phala botswa phalaneng

*The wisdom of the impala shows itself
in the offspring*

Before long, Mama was back at church and dragging me there with her. For now, we only attended the early-morning service instead of the three services that we usually sat through every Sunday. It didn't keep the line of women from stopping Mama after the service for a quick catch-up. I sat on the church steps and watched my grandmother and other people socialise.

'By the stripes of Jesus we declare you are healed!' one of Mama's church friends shouted, clutching both of Mama's hands while she prayed.

Three boys were heading into the church building and all of them came to a sudden halt when Minenhle walked by. They gawked. Minenhle saw this and winked at them, flashing a smile. I wished Mama would hurry up. I really needed to get down to Sis' Nozipho's before her salon started filling up. I was getting my hair braided this time and not the usual bantu knots. Arriving at school with long flowing braids would make a bold statement about my new position as a matric student.

'Amen!' Mama said with passion. Finally we could leave.

The salon was already starting to fill up by the time I got there.

'Woza sthandwa sami.' Wearing flowery leggings and a white caftan, Sis' Nozipho matched her outfit to her bright personality. I had to sleep with a wet doek that night but was greeted with compliments on Monday morning.

'So how much does this lady charge to do your hair like that?'

'This was six-fifty,' I said.

'Six hundred and fifty! Uyageza yhu, she's crazy. I do my hair for two hundred. Two-fifty at the most,' one of my classmates remarked.

Sis' Nozipho was a bit pricey, but that didn't stop her salon from filling up on weekends, with no room at all for people to sit at month end. Women who would complain on each salon visit to her would still sit down in her chair and get their hair done and come back again and again. Sis' Nozipho and Dineo liked to say: 'A woman's confidence pours from the head down'. Judging by how good I felt, I was inclined to agree. The pain I was suffering under that taut fibre on my head was all worth it.

* * *

'Have you decided which university you're going to yet?' I asked Sindi during our lunch break.

The stakes were much higher in grade twelve. My dream to study drama had only intensified and I would like to believe that my acting talents were improving with each play I read and with each character I tried to become. I had already chosen the university I wanted to attend.

'University, Naledi?' Sindi was surprised by my question. 'Haibo, just wait a minute, we are still far from that.'

'It's not that far, Sindi – we have to start applying now.'

'Applications are not even open. You seem to forget that not just anyone gets into a university. You have to be smart, extremely smart. Just because your mother has money, you think you will get in. Worry first about passing exams and stop dreaming about universities so early.'

'That's why I've been reading and preparing myself, Sindiswa.'

'You mean you've been reading the same books for the last ten years a million times and that's enough to get you into university? Su'dlala ngami, Naledi,' Sindi said, shaking her head.

Sindi knew that I spent a lot of my time alone reading and rereading the plays and novels Anika had given me. It was frustrating that I couldn't read more because we didn't have a library at school – and even more frustrating because I could bet the schools that Anika had gone to had libraries. To get to the only library in Pimville, I had to take a thirty-minute walk in the opposite direction to home. But there was something about the way that Sindi had mocked my collection of plays and novels that pushed me to take that walk to the library that very same day after school – and every day after that.

Inside, the library was much bigger than I had thought. It

105

was filled with rows and rows of every kind of book you could imagine. I loved the smell and feel of the old books even more than the new ones – not that there were many new books. I would spend an hour lost in that space that was so quiet it made me forget that I was in a noisy township.

Then I would run back to get home before raising my grandmother's suspicions. Of course the walk there wasn't so bad, but Mama would never allow me to walk that far. Every area outside of Zone 2 was a murder capital according to her.

There was a lot riding on me now. I was at the age when my mother had fallen pregnant with me. A few weeks into the term, Mama reminded me about the curse.

We both sat on the bed preparing to pray. As usual she faced the window.

'Has Dineo called since the last time she was here?' Mama asked.

'No, Mama,' I said.

Instead of asking me to recite the scripture, Mama raised a finger and said, 'You know it says, *Every sin that a man doeth is without the body; but he that committeth fornication sinneth against his own body.* You see a weak woman by how hard she leans on a man, even defiling her own body, not because of his loving heart but because of how deep his pockets are. She is weak because she fails to see that she could stand upright on her own, in her own God-given capacity. You must fight, Naledi. My mother was a servant and so was I and so is your mother. The only difference is that my mother and I were servants to white people while your mother is a servant to sin. Naledi, you must *flee fornication*!'

My grandmother always knew how to strike fear in me. It worked every time.

Ukufunda akupheli, kuphela amalanga

*Learning never ends,
it's the days (of living) that end*

It was a Tuesday night probably just after eleven o'clock. Mama and I were woken up by a scream that cracked our walls. We heard feet hitting the ground followed by footsteps stomping through our yard.

'It's definitely not a person from around here. No one here would try to steal from me,' Mama muttered.

We heard a knock.

Mama ran to the door, still dressed only in her nightgown and doek.

'Mama Norah, please come.' It was Lolo, rushing through his words. I sat up in bed, listening to them speaking over the thudding of my heart. I felt it in every muscle and trace of blood in my body. That same sickening feeling I had when I watched my grandmother lying helpless in bed. The hairs on my arms were standing up and my limbs were cold.

Three hours later, Mama returned. She sat on the bed as we listened to MaKarabo's cries from next door that crept through our thin walls. I knew what Mama was about to say. I had known that the day was near but I allowed her to speak anyway. After a long silence the words eased out of her mouth.

'Karabo has left us,' she said.

I slipped back down into bed, covered myself with the blankets and slept.

The day before Karabo's funeral arrived. When the sun came up, I woke up and prepared for school like I did on any other ordinary morning. Reality had set in.

I knew I was dragging my feet along the tar, but everything felt so heavy that carrying my schoolbag on my back, that carrying my own body, was not without great effort.There'd be no trip to the library today. I walked straight out of the school gates and headed home.

When I turned into Ndende Street, a guy in his late twenties stood in the middle of the empty white tent that had been erected in the street outside of the Moloi household. He was having a full-blown argument with himself. The kids who filled our street pointed and laughed.

'Voetsek, nina!' one woman who was walking into Ma-Karabo's busy yard chastised them.

'Nyaope boys' is what Mama called them. The closer I walked towards him, the more familiar he seemed. He opened his mouth and stretched out his arms wide, as if he wanted to embrace me. 'Uh, my sista,' he said and smiled with brown teeth. That nyaope boy was Thabiso – Clement's friend who always sat drinking under the tree with him on the old car seat. His face and lips had darkened, while his frame had become much smaller and more sunken. He began to tango through the street, jeered at by every little boy and girl who had paused their game of black mampatile to watch the dance unfold. The comedy ended abruptly. The woman who had sworn at those kids for laughing was right, that sort of thing wasn't funny at all. I had never really cared much for Thabiso nor given him a second thought, but I walked into the house with my heart slipping deeper into pain.

Mama called me to come to help out. I almost spilt the hot water all over the kitchen table when I saw Karabo's body being carried in. Everyone around the house stood up as the women in their long dresses and doeks ushered in the coffin with Sesotho hymns. The coffin was placed in the bedroom where MaKarabo and two of her sisters were sitting on a mattress on the floor.

The lady who was leading the songs had the sharpest and shakiest soprano I had ever heard in my life. I turned to look at the big blown-up picture of Karabo smiling that had been placed among the wreaths in the living room, and none of it felt right. The horrible singing, MaKarabo's constant screams, her being carried out of the bedroom to breathe, the confusion on Karabo's daughter's face, and my standing there knowing that inside that wooden box those men had brought in was where my dead friend lay . . . Lord Jesus, surely you knew too that it was all wrong.

When I got back to our house, long after midnight, my feet hurting from standing and serving tea and cookies and washing endless dishes, I collapsed into my bed. Mama barely slept and only came back to bath and get dressed in the morning before hurrying back next door.

Outside in the street, flowing out of the tent, there were more than three buses' worth of people. We left for the cemetery with Lolo and his uncles carrying out the coffin. The Apostolic Church choir was dressed in uniform. They sounded nothing like the women who had come over the night before. The choir sang without the razzmatazz of instruments, just the purity of their voices reverberating through the air. They looked like a host of angels standing near the grave.

Once they had sealed her body in the ground, everyone rushed off to their cars, the buses packed with bodies, because a plate of food and beers for the after tears awaited them. Even over someone's death, the people around here felt it necessary to blast music, dance and get drunk.

I stood in front of my older sister's grave and thought about our permanent goodbye. I thought back to the days when we used to giggle like naughty schoolgirls, when she would pass me magwinya or kgogo through the fence. I remembered her parents' living room with her teasing me about Sihle. I laughed.

As I took a fistful of the heap of soil, feeling its soft texture. It slipped through my fingers and onto her grave. Karabo was gone.

It felt like a cold hand took hold of my heart and was squeezing it too tightly. I gasped for air and felt my knees hit hard against the ground. There was a warm touch on my shoulder. I looked up and it was Lolo. He stretched out his hand and I took hold of it as he pulled me up. He placed his arms around me. I pressed my head against his chest, listening to the pounding of his heart. Finally, I shed tears.

Bana ba sekolo, bana ba sekolo tloong sekolong

*Schoolchildren, schoolchildren,
come to school*

Mama came in from sweeping, carrying a letter. I made her tea, then sat down to eat my porridge. Mama slid the letter across the table towards me. I scrutinised the white envelope before opening it. It was from the university, giving a date for my audition. I broke out in a smile. I hadn't smiled in a long time.

Before the arrival of that letter, I had stopped standing at the gate. There was nothing much to see on Ndende Street; there was nothing to look forward to. I hadn't hidden myself behind the toilet to write in my journal either. There was a lot to write about, but actually penning the words felt too arduous a task.

Holding that letter in my hands, I took a deep breath in and exhaled.

'God hears us when we pray,' Mama said.

I headed for the library that following Monday after school. I needed to catch up on the reading I had neglected. I needed to find more plays and ensure that I would be fully prepared for my audition.

Sindi was standing with Sihle by the main road. That was weird. But it was *how* they were standing that really flummoxed me.

Close. Too close.

Sindi was smiling, while Sihle caressed her face. They walked off, Sihle's arm wrapped around Sindi's waist and Sindi's head leaning on his shoulder. I never made it to the library that day.

Sindi arrived just in time for assembly. She greeted me casually while we stood in line, as she did every other day, knowing full well what she had been doing behind my back all along.

'Hao, Naledi, I'm greeting you. Why are you ignoring me?' Sindi whispered from behind me.

'Baba wethu osezulwini.' I closed my eyes, pressing my palms tightly together and prayed louder than everyone else. I needed all the strength I could get from God to help me deal with Sindi.

She continued to poke me in my back. 'Psst, Naledi!'

'Njengoba nathi sibathethelela abasonayo.' I turned my head to face her as I said that part of the Lord's Prayer. She didn't pick up that I was directing the words to her. Clearly she didn't feel an ounce of guilt for trespassing against me and yet I knew that God still expected me to forgive her.

I couldn't ignore her forever, and by the time break came around, she had grown tired of my game of silence and demanded answers.

'I saw you with Sihle yesterday by the main road, close to Pimville Square!' I was livid.

Sindi just stared at me and nonchalantly said in her Sindi kind of way, 'Manje?'

I placed my hands on my hips and stared back at her.

'Sindi, I saw you holding hands with Sihle!'

Sindi slowly folded her arms across her chest and tilted her head slightly.

'Naledi, have you and Sihle ever dated?'

'No.'

'Have you ever kissed him?'

'No.'

'Have you ever had sex with him?'

'Sies, Sindiswa!' I shouted. Where did that question come from? Why would she even go so far as to ask me something like that?

'Because I have.'

With just those three words, Sindi destroyed me. My knees suddenly turned to jelly. I could see the satisfaction on her face as she continued: 'Nothing has ever happened between you and Sihle so I don't see the problem, ukuthi siyajola. I didn't tell you because I didn't want to hurt you.'

I walked away from Sindi and knew at that moment that it was over. This was the second friend I'd have to bury.

* * *

The university of my dreams was much bigger than I had imagined. Mama and I circled the premises a few times trying to find our way. Thankfully, we had woken up at five to ensure that we left the house by six, to make it in time for my audition. We soon realised that we had gone to the main campus by mistake. The Arts campus was much smaller, with a lot more graffiti splashed on the walls. Mama's forehead creased. I knew exactly what she was thinking.

'Tea is being served in the cafeteria,' a lady said, tapping my grandmother on the shoulder with her pen while holding on to a clipboard in her other hand. The cafeteria was buzzing with people, mostly parents. I did what many of the other young people were doing: I left Mama and went to explore on my own. People were moving about with instruments and big art portfolio bags, making their way to the different audition spaces.

I saw ten white girls standing in a row with buns on their heads, dressed in their pink tutus and point shoes. Further down the corridor were more dancers in leotards stretching their bodies in ways I never knew possible. I was lost again.

I found another building full of painters in front of canvases, focused on creating their masterpieces. I stopped for a second, looking through the window. There was a man sitting in the front of the class. Everything was hanging out in the open . . . Everything! I had never seen a naked man in my life. Nearly blinded by what I had just seen, I concentrated on finding where I was supposed to be.

'You need to go to the theatre,' someone directed me after I resorted to asking for help. I followed the signs and walked into a big amphitheatre with burgundy-coloured velvet seats. On stage stood a girl, commanding the attention of everyone in the room, belting out notes that awakened every nerve in my body. I still had a few minutes to spare so I stood at the back of the theatre and watched.

'Hi, sorry, there's another theatre, a studio theatre on the other side where the drama people are,' the girl who had directed me earlier came up behind me and explained. She ushered me out and around the corner where other would-be drama students were sitting. Everyone was reciting lines and some even had costumes on. To me, it felt like something straight out of a scene from the movie *Fame*. It was surreal – and I had found home. I sat down with my palms sweating waiting to be called in.

I walked into the audition room. Five blank, unfriendly faces stared back at me. I could feel my heart jumping out of my chest.

'Give us your name and what you're going to perform,' a white old lady with glasses positioned almost on the tip of her nose said.

I took centre stage in an all-black theatre space. I was barefoot and dressed in all black like the books I had read had advised. This was the moment I had been preparing for for so many years.

'Kwena, Naledi Kwena. I'll be performing a monologue from *You Strike a Woman, You Strike a Rock* written by Phyllis Klotz, Poppy Tsira, Thobeka Maqhutyana and Nomvula Qosha.'

I was ready.

* * *

The final weeks leading to the end of the school calendar were very exciting, and the mood was jovial. But it was strange for me because amid all of that I didn't see much of Sindi.

She had missed three of our final exams. Sindi was many things but not that reckless.

When December came around, so did Dineo with bags of groceries and an unusually cheerful spirit. She scooped me up in her Porsche and we spent a full day going in and out of different stores buying everything and anything I wanted – a cellphone, laptop, backpack, exam pads, pens, and lots of clothes.

'You must show that you are a university student. You are not like the rest of them on Ndende Street. Re kgalema lenyatso.'

Was Dineo actually proud of me, I wondered.

I wondered about Mama too. I had been accepted into the university provisionally, and was just waiting until my final results came out. The wait was long. I was filled with anxiety on most days. Everyone in our street knew that I was in matric: even Clement was interested.

'Sho, Naledi, vede?' he greeted from across the street where he was sitting.

'Hayi ke sharp, Clement, wena?' I greeted back as I polished the windowsills.

'Hayi ke grand, mfethu. Jwanong, when are the results coming out?' he asked.

'On the second,' I informed him.

'Oho. I heard that you going to university. Sho ngwana – well done.' Clement got up from his old car seat and started applauding me.

118

It felt good to have so many people excited about this new step – as if this small achievement was an achievement for all of us in this community.

The morning of 2 January, Mama and I were woken up by Lolo knocking roughly on our front door. He had scaled the fence. I beat Mama to the door this time.

Lolo grabbed me by the hand and off we went. Lolo didn't care that I still had on my nightdress and pantyhose on my head. We ran to the shops where a number of people had converged, waiting for the shop owner to open so that they could buy the newspaper. We finally got our hands on one and placed it on the ground, flipping the pages looking for the section where all the people whose surnames starting with 'K' were written. Lolo scrolled down and there it was: 'Kwena, Naledi'. Lolo jumped up and shouted. I stood there crying. He picked me up, spun me around, then squeezed me tightly and kissed me on my forehead.

We found Mama outside, also in her nightdress with just a towel wrapped around her waist. She was with MaKarabo and Ntate Moloi. Lolo shouted from the street corner, 'She passed!'

As soon as we entered our yard, Mama raised her hands to the heavens and began praying speedily in tongues. MaKarabo drenched me in a shower of adulation. It was Ntate Moloi who properly looked at the paper and informed us that I had passed with five distinctions.

I ran to the house to get my brand-new cellphone to call my mother. Her phone just kept ringing. *Mxm!* I gave up.

Lolo walked me to school in the afternoon to fetch my report card. The entire walk to school, people stopped and asked, 'Naledi, did you pass?' Everyone asked – from Felicia, a lady from church, to Sis' Nozipho, who even offered to do my hair free of charge to get me ready for university.

I got my results but Sindi was still nowhere to be found.

'Was her name in the paper?' Lolo asked.

'No, I didn't see it.'

'Let's hope she doesn't go drinking Halephirimi or even hanging herself,' Lolo said.

I couldn't be annoyed with him, because that was always the first thought that crept into people's minds when people heard that someone didn't pass matric. People did sometimes go that far, and hanging and rat poison were the popular choices.

Lolo and I ran into the nose-bleeding Siyabonga at the school gate. I thought maybe he would have had an idea about Sindi since he was Sihle's friend.

'Uh uhambile uSindi. Her mother shipped her back to KZN to her grandmother when she found out that she was pregnant. She didn't tell you?' Siyabonga's eyes widened with shock that I was clueless about something of that magnitude.

'No, she didn't,' I said.

I was amazed to see the Porsche parked outside our house. Dineo had bought food and cake to celebrate. It had been years since Mama and Dineo and I had sat down at that table together. MaKarabo, Ntate Moloi, Lolo and Nthabi joined us, but I secretly struggled to stay in my euphoric mood: the news of Sindi still weighed on my heart.

NALEDI

'O Jola le mang wa ma Top 7'

Who are you dating?

I was sitting outside the cafeteria on the wide stretch of green lawn, biting into my two slices of brown bread spread with peanut butter and jam. An engrossingly vulgar exchange of words was taking place in front of me. A group of about nine guys were all huddled up closely in a circle. Some had mohawks and others high-top haircuts, and were wearing seriously low-hanging jeans, in an effort to show off their scotch-patterned briefs, I presumed.

One of them created the beat with his mouth and, two at a time, they would hurl lyrical insults and F-bombs at each other to the adulation of the rest who were listening. There was something poetic in the way they would deliver their punch-lines, with the words flowing out of their mouths as if without much thought.

I never seemed to come out of class early enough to find a vacant table or bench. All the tables were always occupied by little cliques or by the guitar boy. I was sitting about two feet away from him. There were two things I had already gathered about this guitar boy with the tattoos and long dreadlocks that swept over his face: one, he was obsessed with Stevie Wonder, and two, he was never in class.

Rain or shine, I always found him sitting at the exact same spot, with his feet on the chair and butt on the table, strumming his guitar for whoever cared to listen.

I buried my nose further in the script I was trying to memorise for my acting class. Seeing everyone around me with weird fashion choices, sitting and laughing in groups, highlighted not only how different I was but also how alone I was. I was actually missing Sindi terribly. How had I lost my two best friends by the time I had finished school?

'It's her birthday – please sing her something,' a girl said to Guitar Boy, dragging two friends behind her.

'What's your favourite song?' Guitar Boy asked the birthday girl.

'Anything by Zonke,' she said.

'I don't really listen to Zonke. But I can play you something much better,' Guitar Boy said, gliding his fingers along the strings. Closing his eyes, he began to sing, '*So long for this night I prayed, that a star would guide you my way.*'

I wasn't at all surprised that Guitar Boy had chosen to sing 'Ribbon in the Sky'. It was either that or 'Happy Birthday'. His other favourite was 'My Cherie Amour', but he had sung that two days ago to a girl I think he quite liked. Whenever the raven-haired girl walked by, he would break out into song, keeping his gaze fixed on the Indian beauty.

'Naledi?' a voice came from behind me.

122

Standing over me was the most dangerously striking body I'd ever come across. Even with her long relaxed hair combed neatly into a bun, I could recognise that hair anywhere. There wasn't another black girl I knew with hair that rich. She wore a pink leotard and nude ballet stockings which didn't leave much to the imagination.

She sat down, placing her bag on the ground. 'You are Mme Norah's granddaughter, aren't you? Ligama lami nguMinenhle.'

I said nothing but continued to stare at her.

'I know its usual for a Swati girl to be named Minenhle, but I actually just prefer to be called Minnie. Ngiyajabula kukwati. Oh, and this is my roommate, Itu,' she said.

I almost didn't notice Minnie's roommate, I was so distracted by the poise and beauty she possessed up close.

'Do you know how to play anything else besides the three Stevie Wonder songs you torture us with every day?' Itu had a smart mouth.

'Oh, her bark's far worse than her bite,' Minnie added, seeing the stunned look on my face at Itu's remark to poor Guitar Boy. 'I saw you on the first day and thought that there was no way that that could be *the* Mme Norah's granddaughter. But your hair – you've had the same hairstyle for as long as I've seen you at church so I knew it had to be you. Who knew that Mme Norah could raise an artist. She seems so, you know, so—'

'Narrow-minded?' Itu cut Minnie short.

'No, Itu. I was gonna say conservative,' Minnie quickly tried to explain herself.

'And what's the difference?' Itu said, throwing down a thick textbook with the title *African Art*, Steve Biko's *I Write What I Like* and a thinner novel on top of two books by Chinua Achebe. She sat down across from Minnie, placing me very uncomfortably in the middle of their debate.

'The one is intolerant while the other is just a traditionalist.'

'I find that tradionalists are often intolerant people.'

'That's not always true, Itu,' Minnie said, digging her hand into her backpack and pulling out a lighter and a pack of cigarettes. She perched a cigarette between her lips and lit it before casually asking, 'You don't mind me smoking, do you, Naledi?'

Of course I minded! What was she doing? She was Moruti's daughter and here she was passing smoke through her lips like someone who had done this many times before.

'I'm Itumeleng, but most people just call me "Itu",' Itu said, interrupting my train of thought.

Now that Itu was sitting so close to me, my eyes began to notice the many things about her that were out of the ordinary. The big gold ring hanging from her septum, another on her tongue and five along her right ear. They almost made her platinum-blonde hair seem like a mild choice of colour for a dark-skinned black girl.

'Naledi,' I said shaking her hand, 'although people often call me "Ledi".'

That was a lie. I had only been called Ledi by my old crush who had ended up getting my best friend pregnant, but I needed as many things as possible to help me seem like I could keep up with everyone else in this strange new world.

'Ledi. I like that, it's very cute,' Minnie said.

I'm not sure if Minnie was aware that the smoke from her cigarette was moving in my direction or not. It smelt terrible, but worse than that, I didn't want that terrible smell on my clothes. How would I explain coming home and smelling like a chimney to Mama? *Blend in, Naledi; smile and act normal.*

Over time it became easier. Whenever I found myself alone on the lawn outside the cafeteria waiting for either Itu or Minnie, I would sit on the table next to Guitar Boy, singing along with him: 'La la la la la la, la la la la la la'. The unspoken deal was that I would start the song and let him sing the rest on his own when his crush walked by. His name was Lwandle, but he didn't mind the three of us referring to him as 'Guitar Boy'.

Just like Minnie, I began to carry body spray in my bag and would spritz large amounts of it over my clothes before going home. I had fallen in love with Itu's Afropunk sense of style. I also stopped questioning why we chose to communicate in English when all three of us were in fact black. Mama told MaKarabo that I spoke English like I was passing it through my nose. She said that with pride in her voice. Instead of saying, 'Nnyaa,' to Mama, I would say, 'No'. And when I introduced myself to people, instead of saying, 'Liena lame ke Naledi,' I would say instead, 'My name is Ledi'. That's how people knew me now – Ledi.

*   *   *

125

Four o'clock on a Friday, my favourite time. This was when campus was the most quiet. It gave me at least an extra hour to rehearse before having to rush home before dark. Right now, I needed the extra time because I was struggling to get into the emotions of the character I'd been given for my first exam. I was wishing that I could burn the script when a song began to echo through the hallway.

I had thought the department was deserted. But someone else was there. The song played on and, without knowing how, I found myself being carried along with its chords. And as if pulled by the melody, out flowed my monologue.

I had to find out who my collaborator was. I walked down the hall, my feet chasing the music, and there he was: smooth brown skin, bow legs and a chiselled jaw. He stood in the middle of the empty room, blowing hard into the saxophone like the winds of August.

My heart leapt. I pressed my lips together after feeling my bottom lip softening from the tingling sensation that was moving over it. Butterflies were dancing in my stomach. This boy was more beautiful than the music he was playing. This was sin; I knew that. I needed to stop – and I did just that. I shoved the script into my bag and left.

It became a routine over the next few weeks – my practising to his music. Each time I rehearsed my monologue over the beautiful sounds of the saxophone, I felt myself becoming one with the text. Together, the music and words removed me from the room I was rehearsing in and put me in a space where I could feel every emotion in my heart, and the weight of it on my body.

'Damn, you're amazing,' the voice came from behind me.

Every word in the Setswana and English languages left me. I was a nervous mute, standing in front of my collaborator.

'I'm sorry for disturbing you. I was walking past and was so gripped by you, I had to watch. You were so into it you didn't even hear me come in. I've also just finished rehearsing.'

When I opened my mouth to speak, nothing came out. 'I, I, um . . .'

'My name is Sizwe, by the way.'

I nodded instead of saying, '*No, you didn't disturb me. I love how you play the saxophone. Your music has actually helped me with my own piece. Oh, and I'm Ledi.*' All I did was to stare at him, the words stuck in my throat.

'I'm gonna let you carry on doing what you were doing,' he said as he turned to walk away.

Lolo was walking home with his soccer boots slung over his shoulders. He was wearing his soccer jersey half on, half off, exposing part of his torso. His shoulders were getting broader, matching his tall frame. He had a slight bounce in his gait and his abs were as ripe as his hormones – something that did not escape the girls he passed.

'Lolo, come here.'

'Lolo, you still owe me a visit.'

'Hi, Lolo.'

'Lolo, I'm gonna come to your street later, neh.'

'If you wore your top properly, you wouldn't draw so much attention, you know,' I advised Lolo, who feigned his irritation at every girl who tried to flirt with him.

'I'm hot, Naledi. I've been running and kicking a ball, and this top is sweaty,' he said, trying to come up with reasons why he couldn't wear his soccer jersey like a normal person. 'Entlek keng ka wena vandag? Are your periods eating you?' he said.

'Excuse me?'

'You're moody, jo. Your energy is just heavy on me today,' Lolo continued.

I walked away from him, increasing my pace with each step. Lolo ran behind me, trying to apologise until we reached home.

'Leave me alone. I don't want to talk to you!'

'Naledi, wait, sheba askies,' Lolo pleaded, grabbing my arm. I wrestled myself free each time he took hold of me.

MaKarabo and Mama were standing in their yards and talking to each other across the fence. MaKarabo shouted, 'Lolo, what are you doing to Naledi?'

Lolo finally let go of me and I slipped into my yard.

I greeted my grandmother, then MaKarabo, who, instead of saying hello, asked, 'What's wrong with the two of you, keng na, la jola?'

Lolo laughed but it wasn't funny. Why would MaKarabo ask me if I was Lolo's girlfriend and, worse, do that in front of my grandmother?

'He, e, he, e, MaKarabo, don't come and say such things. Naledi is not that kind of a girl!' Mama said.

Seeing how upset my grandmother was, MaKarabo became apologetic. 'No, I was just asking fela because you see how these two carry on.'

'Nnyaa, MaKarabo! What you should be doing is watching Lolo and the way *he* carries on lately. Leave Naledi out of this!'

Mama flounced towards the house. I followed.

Back inside the house, Mama seemed even more livid.

'Le wena o busy running around like a loose girl in the streets with boys! It's dangerous and reckless. You forget that you are a child of God. You are throwing yourself right into the pit of temptation. If I catch you running around with Lolo again, I'm going to kill you both!' she said, slamming the tea things on the table.

Mama had a way of exaggerating everything. I was in no way tempted by Lolo.

*   *   *

I was coming from the theatre and from a distance could see Itu standing in front of Guitar Boy. My eyes landed on Minnie. Strangely, Itu and Guitar Boy seemed not in the least bit bothered.

The guy Minnie was with must have been in third or fourth year. He was not just kissing Minnie; he had his tongue thrust inside Minnie's mouth for a really unnecessary length of time. I had seen many people put their bedroom affections out in public before; this was nothing new. But I guess I still had it in my head that just the previous Sunday, Minnie had been dressed in a pretty floral dress that went over her knees, stand-

129

ing in the pulpit with the holy book in her hand, giving a word for the offering. Not just anybody got to stand in the pulpit, never mind do the offering in our church.

The guy planted his lips on the side of her neck. When he did this, Minnie tilted her head upwards and slightly to the left. Her eyes closed, and she smiled broadly, giggling.

'Ledi, are you okay?'

'Huh? Oh, yes, yes, no, I'm fine. Hey, guys,' I said.

The Indian beauty walked by, drawing our attention to her. By now she had gathered that Guitar Boy was in love with her and I think she quite liked hearing the song which at that point was starting to get on my nerves.

'I don't get it. With *sooo* many black single beautiful girls on campus, you go chasing after an Indian girl?' Itu remarked, rolling her eyes at Guitar Boy.

'I'm not into black chicks,' Guitar Boy said, shrugging.

I had never taken an interest in the guy, so whom he liked was his business as far as I was concerned. Itu, on the other hand, was appalled.

'What!'

'And what's wrong with black girls?' Minnie jumped into the conversation too.

A part of me even appreciated Guitar Boy's statement because it got Minnie to stop making out indecently with that boy.

'Black girls have too much self-hatred, from the fake hair, fake eyelashes, now fake asses and constantly fighting and competing with one another for a man, I just can't,' Guitar Boy explained.

130

'That's rich coming from a black African singer who only has American songs in his repertoire,' Itu shot back.

'Stevie Wonder is still black, Itu, and that's not even what we are talking about. This is about black women and their inability to stand proudly in their own skin. Why must you guys put a white woman's hair on your head to feel beautiful?'

Itu was boiling.

'When Kourtney is sitting under the sun for hours and goes for spray tans trying to darken her skin, nobody says anything to Kourtney, but wait until Khetiwe tries to lighten her skin. When Kourtney puts on hair extensions, fake lashes and gets a nose and boob job, Kourtney is so sexy, but when Khetiwe does it, she's not proud to be an African woman. When Kourtney wears hot pants, it's understandable because it's thirty-two degrees outside, but when Khetiwe wears hot pants she has no self-respect. When Kourtney gets raped, we say, "Ag, man, shame, which monster would do such a thing," and when Khetiwe gets raped, we ask, "Where was she and what was she wearing?" When Kourtney stands up to assert herself, Kourtney is smart and independent. But Khetiwe is just angry and bitter.'

Itu moved closer to Guitar Boy, eyeballing him. 'The enemy of the black woman will always be the black man,' she said, then picked up her bag and sauntered off.

* * *

I hadn't told my friends about Sizwe, mainly because I couldn't believe that someone as splendid as him had noticed me, umnyamane, as Xolani would say. So when Sizwe stood like a beautiful framed picture in the doorway later on in the afternoon, I was beyond flustered.

'Hey,' he said.

'Hey,' I said back to him.

'You still haven't told me your name, you know.'

'I . . . I . . .' I stammered. 'Ahem,' I cleared my throat and told myself to breathe. 'My, my name is Ledi . . . Ledi, which is short for Naledi.'

He looked down at his palms, and bit his bottom lip. Nodding four times, he then looked up at me and remarked, 'Your name is as cute as you are.'

I swear my cheeks turned a different colour, even though science would argue that it was impossible for a dark-skinned girl to change colour when she blushed. Sizwe defied science. He had the ability to add life and emotion into a text he wasn't a part of. He could be in the centre of a play in which he had no character.

He took a seat by the window. 'You don't mind if I watch, right?'

I shook my head, *No*, then stood in the centre of the room. He watched me as he listened, his eyes piercing.

I went to sit next to him by the window when I was done. He began to speak and I just smiled, pretending to be listening. I was too distracted by his brown eyes, his pink moving lips and the expressions on his face. His hand landed on my thigh. Once that happened, I heard nothing else. After a while, his voice became audible to my ears again.

'As an artist, you must make the audience feel something whether it is anger or nostalgia or pain or even love. You have to move me with what you do, uyang'thola,' he said fervently.

'Yes, definitely, you're right.'

I probably would have agreed with anything that came out of Sizwe's mouth. But what he said seemed to be exactly what I needed to hear as I stood on that black-painted stage delivering my first exam to the audience of students the following day. I thought back to our conversation and I could hear the sound of his saxophone playing in my ear. It was another memorable performance from me and my collaborator.

*　*　*

People often joked that because schools were closed, so were the taps. Children played all day and had to be reminded by their parents to come back home and take a bath. Thabiso would show up asking for money from anyone he saw walking by. Clement chilled under the tree with a cigarette in his hand, and like me, he would watch the busy bodies of Ndende Street go about their lives.

Felicia and Thiza would spend hours standing at the corner outside of Felicia's house talking. They would walk down to the shops to kiss each other away from the glaring eyes of the people on our street, especially away from Felicia's grandfather. Whichever kid had seen them kissing by the shops would then come back to the rest of the gang to report the tale: 'Tjo tjo, ke ba bone ba sunana, they were kissing outside the Somalian man's shop.'

133

Mama proceeded to move every single piece of furniture, and then on my knees I went to strip the tiles clean before polishing them. With the curtains hanging along the fence, the view of Ndende Street was broader from inside our home. Lolo entered his parents' yard and was met by an angry Ma-Karabo. It was odd seeing MaKarabo shouting like that. She was always so cheerful.

'Lolo, keng mara? What is this rubbish I am hearing about you being busy with Nozipho?'

There was a rumour about Lolo and Sis' Nozipho having an indecent affair spreading like wild fire through our street, so much so that I was beginning to believe the tale even though it had sounded ridiculous to me at first. There were even more rumours – and these I believed – that her husband had had a baby with another woman.

'Nka jola le mme mara? C'mon!' Lolo shouted. 'Do you see how old she is and you are gonna stand there and ask me such a thing?'

'Why would people just make up a story like that?' Ma-Karabo yelled.

'You know the people ba mo Zone 2 are always talking rub-bish!' Lolo defended himself.

MaKarabo walked away.

'Sies, you know Lolo has no self-respect. He doesn't even feel an ounce of compassion for his parents who have had to bury their child because of this thing of running around with this person and that person,' Mama hissed. 'Wena, Naledi, if I see you standing and talking to that boy, you will know me!'

For those reasons alone, I had started to look forward to Sundays. Minnie and I sat together inside the empty church building after attending all three services.

'So you want him?' Minnie asked with a mischievous grin on her face.

'Eish, I really don't know,' I said to her because the truth was that I had no idea what I wanted from Sizwe. I also had never been in any kind of a relationship so I wasn't sure how any of it worked, or if Sizwe was even interested in me.

'Yoh kodzwa, Sizwe is hot,' Minnie said thoughtfully.

'That he is . . .' I pictured him standing in front of me.

'The things I would do to—'

'Sies, Minnie, what do you mean?'

'Ow, Ledi, nawe, don't act so innocent.'

'I like the guy – that's about it, Minnie.'

'So you just want to stare at him, that's it? You don't want to kiss him and you've never imagined him holding you?' Minnie asked suspiciously.

I looked at the huge wooden cross that hung on the altar in front of us and immediately rebuked myself for my sinful thoughts. 'This is not right, Minnie,' I said to her eyeing the cross.

'There's nothing wrong with a kiss, Ledi. There's no place in the Bible where it says, *Thou shall not kiss and develop-est feelings for a boy*.'

'But the Bible is very clear about fornication.'

'Kissing is fornication now? Hayi bo friend, please, relax – it's not that deep.'

135

I was glad when Mama walked in and told me that we were leaving. Minnie had given me a lot to think about.

Mama couldn't hide how happy she was that I had become such good friends with the pastor's daughter.

'So she does this acting thing with you at school?' Mama asked as we made our way home.

'No, she's a ballet dancer.'

'Sho, bar-lay! Kante there are black people who know how to do barlay? Moruti and Mamoruti are raising a true leader, ka nnete.'

Leoto ke moloi

The foot is a witch

The first day back on campus was the usual scene of screaming girls who ran up to one another and hugged as if they were old relatives who had spent decades apart.

'Chomi!' I screamed, bolting towards Itu. Nothing much had changed about Itu except for her platinum-blonde hair which was now a Persian-blue colour.

'I'm dying over your hair,' I said. Itu did a quick spin.

'Where's Minnie?' I asked.

'She had ballet at seven this morning. She's almost done, though,' Itu said, leading the way to the cafeteria. We sat down at our usual spot, coffees in hand.

When Minnie arrived she immediately began scratching through her bag. She placed a pamphlet on the grass in front of us.

Spring Bash 2017 was written in bold, with the names of a number of big-time musicians and DJs in the background.

'Ja, I don't think I can go, guys,' I said. 'My grandmother would never allow me.'

Itu stopped her excited dance.

'Ledi, do you honestly think that I'm going to tell my parents that I won't be coming home on that particular weekend because I'll be out all night partying at the Spring Bash?' Minnie was stern. 'Lie to your grandmother, friend, come on! We're gonna sneak you into our room, and you can spend the weekend with us.'

'You're an actress, Ledi. Surely you can come up with a creative story to feed your grandmother,' Itu said.

Itu and Minnie were not letting this one go. According to Minnie we had not yet fully experienced what it meant to be in tertiary education. I wasn't even aware that there were important things about varsity outside of getting a degree.

'I mean, we haven't even been out clubbing yet. That's just sad, guys,' said Minnie.

I eventually gave in, but the situation made me very uncomfortable. The lying part made me nervous but it was actually the idea of being at a party with hundreds of drunk people dancing uncontrollably that put me completely on edge.

* * *

'Minnie is attending a Youth Bible Camp for a weekend and asked me to go with her.'

This was the lie that I hoped would get me to the party.

The idea of a Youth Bible Camp enthralled Mama. She hummed as she knelt down in the bathroom doing the laundry. She sang softly as she ironed later on in the evening. With the days leading up to the camp, Mama grew more curious. She brought up more and more questions that forced me into creating more lies.

'Jwanong, Naledi, does a camp not need money?'

'I spoke to Dineo and she gave me money to pay for it.'

'I hope she also gave you pocket money.' Mama paused then thought of something else. 'Where did you say this camp is again?'

'Um . . . Somewhere in the Vaal . . .' I was almost impressed by how quickly I thought of that lie. I just hoped that Mama wouldn't mention this camp at church to Moruti or Mamoruti.

* * *

I always listened and Sizwe did all the talking. Half the jazz musicians he made mention of I knew nothing about. But I loved being in his school of music.

We were on the wooden floor of the rehearsal room, staring up at the high ceiling. He was playing 'Tshona!', a song by Pat Matshikiza and Kippie Moeketsi, on repeat. Sizwe analysed the chords and marvelled at the sound. It was a breakaway from talks of varsity bashes and religion.

'Who do you love?' Still lying on the floor, he turned his face towards me.

You, I love being with you – that's what I wanted to say, but I knew that's not what he meant. Besides I wouldn't dare say that to him.

'Anything black, female and it's even better if it's poetic,' I said.

He laughed. 'Basically all things written by Napo Masheane.'

139

'Yeah, pretty much Napo,' I said, giggling.

Sizwe noticed the little things. He had figured out my love for words and even who my favourite playwright was.

Sizwe moved his body closer to mine. He leaned in and kissed me. We kissed for a while, our tongues dancing to 'Tshona!'

I played the song through my headset on the taxi ride home. I played it as I worked on my assignments in the kitchen and in the library on campus. Whenever Itu and Minnie were in class, I'd sit on the grass outside the cafeteria swimming in the sounds of all kinds of dulcet instruments. It was a great song, I thought; it had become *our* song, but it was nothing compared to my new-found favourite.

I paced around the rehearsal room. As soon as I saw Sizwe's face appear through the doorway, I ran to the sound system and let the song play loudly. Sizwe smiled.

'Have you ever heard anything as delicious as this? C'mon, listen to that flugelhorn!' I spoke passionately.

'Babe, you forget that I'm the one who introduced you to Bra Hugh,' Sizwe said.

I paused for a moment, soaking in the fact that he had just called me 'babe'. He walked towards me, held my hands and looked into my eyes.

'"Stimela" is one of the greatest songs I've ever heard, I agree with you,' Sizwe said. 'But why do *you* love it so much?'

Sizwe and I sat on the floor, still holding hands. Something about that space felt safe. I felt like I could grant him permission to see pieces of my heart that I gave no one else access to.

140

'I guess this song reminds me of my grandmother. The story being told in this song is *her* story.'

I began to tell Sizwe about ntatemogolo and how his death had changed Mama into this hard, almost bitter woman. 'I had never realised till that day how broken and angry my grandmother is. I mean, she carries that pain around as if her unwillingness to let go of her anger magically punishes those who hurt her,' I explained.

That day I talked and Sizwe listened. When I was finished, he asked, 'You only ever mention your grandmother. Where are your parents?'

That question altered my mood, though I tried not to show it.

'I don't have a father, and my mother, well, I'm not sure where she is.'

'Everyone has a father, babe, even if we hate to admit it sometimes because they can be so damn useless,' Sizwe said.

'Well, I don't!' I shot out.

Sizwe went quiet. I felt embarrassed that I had just lost my cool like that. Sizwe went on: 'Earlier you said that your grandmother carries anger around as if that will punish those who have hurt her. Don't you think that you're doing the same thing with your parents?'

I took a minute to consider his view. I knew that I was nothing like my grandmother.

'No,' I said softly. 'I say no because I cannot punish the dead.'

Again we were quiet. I had just shown Sizwe my pain,

my past and my heart, something I had never been able to do with anyone else.

I looked out and noticed the sun beginning to set.

'Chill . . . Why are you in such a rush? It's only six,' Sizwe said.

I didn't have time to explain anything or even to say good-bye. I ran as fast as I could to the taxi rank. My grandmother was standing outside the kitchen door, waiting for me.

'Is this the time a girl arrives home?'

'I was finishing my assignment and the library was full, so I had to wait before I could use the internet and my assignment is due tomorrow,' I stammered.

'Nxa!' Mama clicked her tongue and walked into the house.

During my evening bath, I closed my eyes and drifted back to the joy and safety of that rehearsal room. For two hours a day, those four walls were my whole world.

* * *

The res rooms were much smaller than I had imagined. I scanned the room quickly, trying to decide on which side I would settle.

The dirty clothes and the dozens of books scattered along the floor and the bed on Itu's side made Minnie's side the obvious choice. I admired the huge painting Itu had hung above her bed of Winnie Mandela before joining Minnie in sitting on her old single bed.

'Itu, sometimes I feel like you should have studied politics, not art.'

142

'I'm actually joining the SRC soon,' Itu said, throwing her bag down before launching herself onto her messy bed.

Minnie and I shouldn't have been as surprised as we were, but the news did catch us off-guard.

'I don't know, Itu . . . I just feel like these SRC guys are here to cause unnecessary trouble sometimes. Some of us actually want to be in school, and clearly they don't with all these endless nonsense strikes,' Minnie said.

Itu sat up on her bed.

'What makes you think they don't want to study?' she shot back at Minnie. 'You do remember that I spent a night in the streets with a whole lot of other black kids who were also lining up in those NFSAS queues. Because just like me they were stranded and couldn't catch a taxi back to Limpopo. Some of those students still got rejected and those of us who were granted loans will leave this university with debts hanging over our heads before we have even entered the work force. And yet we live in a country that talks about our rights to education and equal education for the black child. The same education that we black children of a democratic South Africa still have to bleed to get. Before you talk shit, walk a mile in the shoes of those who cannot afford anything!'

And with that, the mood in the room had shifted. I resorted to the only thing I knew that would get Minnie and Itu back on loving terms, even though that one thing made me gravely uncomfortable.

'So what are you guys wearing tonight?'

At the mention of the bash, the tension evaporated. Minnie's face lit up. She dashed to her cupboard, pulling out her options.

'So because it's still a bit chilly at night, I'm thinking of these jeans, my crop top and my leather jacket.' Minnie showed us her ensemble for our approval.

Itu and I nodded.

'So what do you guys think I should wear?' I said. Despite dreading actually going to the party, I still wanted to look half decent. 'I've never been to this sort of thing and I want to look good.'

'Look good for who . . . Sizwe?' Itu said dryly, lying back down on her bed. 'Minnie told me about your little afternoon sessions with him.' Minnie giggled, and I blushed. Itu continued: 'Look, I wouldn't be a good friend if I wasn't honest with you. Sizwe is a whore and I can't sit here and pretend to be happy while my friend gets played. Think about it, Ledi, why does he only meet with you after most people have left campus? I'm telling you, this guy's an asshole.'

Minnie headed for the small bar fridge and pulled out a three-litre box of red wine. I could only stomach a single glass but Minnie and Itu's determination to get drunk overpowered the punch of the wine on their palates. Even in their tipsy state, Itu managed to call a taxi and they both seamlessly snuck me out of res with them.

There we were – we'd fallen right into the trap of girlish rapture set by first-time splashes of eyeliner, mascara and lipstick. In my white Converse sneakers, skinny jeans, figure-hugging top and jacket, I couldn't remember a time in my life when I

144

had felt that pretty. Though it could have been the glass of wine I had drunk that had left me feeling a lot more desirable than on my average days.

Clouds of smoke rose above cliques of students huddled up on the large open field puffing and passing joints. Lust was in charge, controlling the raunchy sway in the hips of girls who danced provocatively against the pelvises of thirsty boys. Bottles were raised up towards the heavens, people singing the lyrics of 'Omunye' in a drunken haze.

Minnie soon made the acquaintance of a male stranger, compelling Itu and me to tag along with the pair and the random guy's friends. Leaning against the boot of their car, Minnie talked and smooched with her new friend. Itu got herself a drink from their cooler box. One of the guys passed a cider into my unoccupied hands. Witnessing my internal struggle, Itu shouted above all the different conversations taking place around the old grey Toyota Corolla, 'Ledi doesn't really drink!'

Minnie and her guy stopped kissing. Conversations were halted midway. All heads turned to face me. Some guy said, 'Dude, you don't drink!'

Minnie added, 'Ledi is just good like that – she's never even had sex.'

In her defence, I think she was trying to speak up for me. But I felt a wave of embarrassment. I did not like the taste of alcohol and my reluctance to just suck it up and drink had drawn unnecessary attention. The sex thing, on the other hand, was a far greater burden. Having my virginity still intact felt like I was carrying around a badly infected wound that everyone around me had accidently seen when they were not supposed to.

'Yo, dude, that's incredible – you don't meet virgins any more,' one guy said.

'Yeah, but dating a virgin is hard, man. You virgins get so attached,' another guy added.

'I personally prefer a woman who knows what she's doing. I can't fuck with a virgin. Now I have to teach you and nurse you all at once. Sorry, been there done that,' Minnie's guy weighed in.

'Is this like a religious thing? You know that's all bullshit, right,' another argued.

Again, I think Minnie thought she was helping me: 'No, Ledi is just waiting for the right guy. Right, Ledi?' She looked at me, waiting for a response.

I was mortified. 'I . . . I . . . I . . .'

I stood struggling to come up with a reason as to why I was still a virgin. The rest of the night after that felt too long. I wished I was at home, far from there, in my grandmother's house.

I woke up the next day at around six-thirty and entertained myself by diving into my school work, ignoring the empty McDonald's containers scattered all over the place. Itu and Minnie eventually struggled out of sleep just before noon.

'Where did the McDonald's stuff come from?' Itu asked, holding her head up with her hands.

'You guys bought McDonald's on our way back – don't you remember?' I said.

'Seriously?' Minnie was just as confused.

'Yes, seriously,' I said.

I was shocked that both of them were blank about the previous night. I had seen how drunk they had been, but how was it possible for their memory to be completely wiped out?

'Oh my goodness, but last night was so much fun,' Minnie said and grinned.

'How would you know it was fun if you can't remember much of what happened?' I asked.

'C'mon, Ledi, that's how you know – when you *don't* remember anything,' said Minnie.

'Well, I do remember some parts,' Itu said through a groggy voice. 'I remember you disappearing with that guy.'

Minnie's eyes widened as if images had started flashing in her head. She softly slapped her mouth before adding, 'I think we shagged.'

I did not understand how Minnie would be uncertain about something that important. Surely having sex with someone was not something that could easily slip your mind. It's not like leaving your purse somewhere, but she said it like that; she said it like she was saying, *'I think I forgot my purse in the bathroom.'*

'You *think* you shagged?' I asked.

'Yeah, I think so,' she said it again.

All day, Itu continued to quiz Minnie about her guy, hoping that the questions would help to jog her memory.

147

'I would actually like to meet this guy when I'm sober so that I can rate him, you know,' Minnie said to Itu, who burst out laughing.

Itu and Minnie and even the guys from the previous night treated sex like any other thing, but I knew it wasn't. It was s-e-x. But these events left me questioning myself in a way I had never done before. For a start, how was it that I was the only virgin at the Spring Bash? I hadn't realised that most teenagers walked out of high school *with* a matric certificate and *without* their virginities. Had I been too precious about my virginity?

A hu na muthu a faho a si na tsevhi

*No one dies without having
someone warn them*

Sizwe had asked that we meet in one of the music department rooms. I found him sitting at the piano and took a seat next to him, kissing him before melting into the musicality that ran through his fingers as he began playing Miriam Makeba's 'Ntyilo Ntyilo'. I couldn't stop myself from singing. Soon we found ourselves wrapped up in our usual cheesy romantic musical.

'You didn't tell me that you play the piano!' I looked into his eyes.

'And you didn't tell me you could sing.'

His words made me blush. 'I'm not that great.'

'Take it from a musician, you're not half bad. I, on the other hand, am attempting to become the next Prince, which is why I'm learning to play so many instruments,' he said. 'Anyway, there's something that I've been thinking about.' He swung one leg over the piano chair to turn his body to face me. He held my hands, looked me in the eyes and said, 'I want to make you a woman, Ledi.'

I wondered why he used the term 'a woman' instead of 'my woman'. I understood that there were many things I could learn from Sizwe. He was three years ahead of me and possessed a wealth of knowledge that I got to feed on on a daily basis. But the status of our relationship was still a question mark. He had never come out and asked me to be his girlfriend. Still, the look in his eyes and the gentle tone in his voice led me to nod and say, 'Okay'.

He placed his lips on my forehead, for now removing the confusion his statement had created inside me.

I walked home slowly after getting off the taxi. I was hoping that I would bump into Lolo. Lolo was the only person who could dissect Sizwe's language and hand me the facts that I needed. I heard him opening the gate next door very late when Mama and I were watching *Muvhango*.

'Imagine a child coming back home at this hour during the week,' Mama remarked.

Lolo was hardly a child, I thought. What, was he supposed to stay locked up also, like she had done with me?

* * *

End-of-year exams made our workdays shorter. Sizwe and I would chill in the empty rehearsal room after every exam session. It became *our* place.

Hours would go by and we'd still be talking and laughing. I loved being wrapped up in his arms. I loved it when he would kiss me for no reason at all except that the silence between us at that moment made our lips collide.

One afternoon, Sizwe decided to walk me down to the taxi rank with talk about his township, Alexandra, taking up most of the conversation. He referred to it as 'Gomorrah'. I tried my best to educate him about the real Gomorrah, but I failed. It was all the dark things that happened there that seemed to excite him. 'Kasi yama kasi, the greatest among all ghettos,' he went on.

Sizwe possessed that hard swag that guys from that township had. That hardness may have been diluted by model C schools but even through his polished English, his edge was undeniable.

We were surrounded by a swarm of street vendors, loud-mouthed taxi drivers, commuters and filth at the rank, but all things around me seemed beautiful as I stopped to look at the hazel-eyed boy, with skin the colour of desert sand, who had stolen my heart.

'So what exactly is your plan with us?' I asked finally, making sure that my voice was firm.

Sizwe took one step closer. I looked around trying to see who was looking but he gently took hold of my face. Sizwe didn't care about the elders who were staring at us in disgust. Right then, the moment was between me and him, and no one else.

'Warmth,' and that's all he said before giving me a long kiss goodbye.

I stood there for a minute as he disappeared. I could feel that warmth that he had spoken of tingling in my fingertips and toes. It was as if there was an electric current flowing through me. Mama had made sin sound so vile and grotesque; she had never told me that it felt so good.

* * *

The big end-of-year dance production was set to take place the next day in the amphitheatre on campus. I sat on the steps outside the theatre waiting for Minnie to wrap up her rehearsal. I could hear Ms Anna, her ballet lecturer, drilling her inside the theatre. Sizwe and two of his friends appeared from around the corner. They all walked past, except for Sizwe, who stopped to bend down and greet me.

'Unjani?' he asked, cupping his hand around my cheek.

'Ngiyaphila.'

I always slipped in the very limited isiZulu I had in my vocabulary between my English and Setswana sentences when speaking to Sizwe. I knew without him telling me that he liked hearing me speak his language. He leaned in to kiss me.

'Tomorrow night meet me by the music department, during the interval.'

I smiled. He winked and walked away.

When Minnie collapsed next to me on the steps, I could see that she had worked herself beyond her limits. She was panicking about her big ballet solo tomorrow.

Ms Anna came out. She was a black woman with an athletic build that failed to mask her perfect posture. She looked at Minnie sternly before walking down the stairs.

'You're not going to fail,' I said. I allowed her to rest in my embrace for a little while.

She blinked away her tears. 'I don't want to think about tomorrow. Let's talk about you,' she said.

I told her about my meeting with Sizwe the following day. I must have sounded quite unsure about the whole idea, because she asked, 'What are you scared of?'

'It . . .' I said very slowly.

Minnie took a moment, calculating her words before letting them out. 'It's daunting, I know. I was so young and dumb when I broke my virginity that I really didn't think about what I was actually doing.'

'Do you regret it?'

'What would that help with?' Minnie said. 'What's done is done. I think if you're gonna do it, do it with the right guy. Sex can be painful the first time round, but it hurts even more afterwards if the guy is a complete jerk. The body can take a beating that the heart can't handle, which is why I don't let guys anywhere near my heart.'

The longer Minnie spoke the more stressed I got. I wasn't ready for any kind of pain, whether it was the pain of having a guy pushing his way inside of me or any type of heartbreak for that matter.

'Ledi, relax. Let him take charge. You just need to make sure that you wear matching underwear and keep it smooth, that's all.'

'What do you mean "keep it smooth"?'

'Guys are not into the whole "I keep it natural bush vibe". The only place where a woman is allowed to grow hair is on her head.'

153

'That's ridiculous – if God didn't want women to have hair, hair wouldn't be growing in all the places that it grows.'

'You're spending too much time with Itu; you're starting to sound like her. And besides, are you trying to impress God or Sizwe?'

I had hoped that everything I did in my life would be pleasing to God. This again was a reminder that if I had to do this, I would to have to walk in without God by my side.

Minnie stopped to look at me. 'Are you sure Sizwe is the one?' she asked.

'Can you ever really be sure?'

'No, you can't.'

* * *

I kept thinking back to my conversation with Minnie that night, even during my prayers with Mama. Why did I automatically assume that Sizwe wanted to have sex with me? What stressed me out the most was my inability to say no to Sizwe. I wasn't ready at all to have sex with him, but would I be strong enough to voice how I felt?

'Naledi, keng ka wena?' Mama yelled.

She startled me.

'Huh?'

'We are busy *praying*! Are you no longer afraid of God?'

I was. I was extremely afraid of God and felt so guilty that praying, reciting scriptures and answering Mama's spiritual questions was becoming a heavy task lately.

'I asked you: Rrago ke mang?'

154

'It's God and God alone,' I responded with my voice almost breaking.

I couldn't sleep, so I decided to go do some revision for my exam the next day. I left for class earlier than usual, at seven instead of seven-thirty, hoping that I would see Lolo before catching a taxi, but again, he was nowhere.

I sat in the exam room and couldn't remember the distinct differences between naturalism and realism, for which the essay question on my exam paper asked. I had sat in the kitchen the night before staring blankly at my theatre studies textbook while Mama was sleeping. I walked out of the exam room not feeling good at all.

Before rushing off to get ready for her big performance, Minnie pulled me into the girls' bathroom. She locked us inside one of the cubicles and took out a small plastic container from her backpack.

'Here you go,' she said, pulling out a razor. 'Take it.' She shoved it in my hand, noticing the confused look I had on my face. 'I also got you these.' Minnie dangled a red lace bra and a matching G-string in front of me. 'Remember everything I told you yesterday. Okay, I've got to go. I love you, friend.' She hugged me before speeding out of the bathroom.

I had wondered when the right time would be for a girl to start matching her bra with her panties and even when she should start wearing lace G-strings. It seemed it was the day when she had one of the most important performances of her life and an audience member who eagerly awaited her.

I dropped my boy shorts, placed one leg on top of the toilet seat, and began shaving. It looked strange and new. I had never looked at it in that way before. It wasn't as smooth as Minnie had instructed. I hoped that my inability to get my vagina looking like a little girl's one before puberty wouldn't turn Sizwe off. I packed away my old underwear and buried it at the bottom of my bag. My brand-new matching lace underwear felt light and soft against my skin. The red was striking. It spoke a language of seduction and boldness. I walked out of those bathrooms an imposter.

* * *

Itu knew nothing about my plans with Sizwe. I sat through the first half of the dance production next to her, feeling anxious. Acoustic drums began to beat hard, engulfing the silence in the theatre. I had heard those drums yesterday while Minnie was rehearsing with Ms Anna. Nobody moved and nobody made a sound. The spotlight illuminated Minnie's strong yet feminine frame. She stood on pointes, centre stage. It was not just that Minnie was the only first-year performing a ballet solo; it was that she was the only *black* ballerina with a solo and performing it to live acoustic drums. The audience was putty in her hands.

I could still see the vision of the warrior dancer and hear the pounding of those drums as I snuck off to meet Sizwe. We walked a distance into the dark, to the far end of campus, to his all-male residence. I felt awkward entering the testosterone-filled space. I knew what all the guys who saw me walking in with Sizwe were thinking. Going into Sizwe's room, my nerves reminded me of my vulnerability. Here I was alone in a room with a boy who made me feel funny inside when he touched me.

We sat on the bed in a room full of music sheets, beautiful instruments and a pile of dirty laundry in the corner. Sizwe said nothing; instead, he kissed me, but this time it was different. He played keys with his tongue in my mouth. His lips moved from my lips and down to my neck, still playing with his tongue around the edges of my collarbone. He pulled my T-shirt over my head and off, tossing it to the floor. His hands travelled further down my waist where he eased my leggings off. He paused for a second, staring at my undergarments that barely concealed parts of my half-naked body.

When Sizwe kissed and touched my breasts, I finally understood what he meant on that day when he told me that he wanted to make me a woman. A part of me wanted to tell him to stop, but before I could open my mouth to speak, I was already fully naked, feeling the pressure of his fingers inside of me. He kissed me again as if to rebuke the thoughts of my wanting to put an end to this. The longer his fingers caressed and tugged in and around my wet opening, the more I craved him. He got undressed, standing naked before me. My eyes traced his slim body all the way down to his hands. I watched him open and slip on a condom. I had told myself that I had left God outside of that room, but a voice in my head kept reminding me of Mama's scriptures: *The eyes of the Lord are in every place, keeping watch on the evil and the good.* I couldn't hush Mama's loud voice that was repeatedly saying, 'A girl

157

oils her body and spirit in sin when she spreads her legs for a man before he marries her.' As I was fighting to silence her voice, Sizwe spread my legs further, grabbing my thighs with both his arms and pulled my body down to meet his pelvis. He made his way in, filling every inch of my tight vaginal walls. He pushed in deeper, turning what was a pleasurable feeling just a moment ago into pain that I failed to articulate with words. I knew better than to scream, even though everything inside of me wanted to. My groaning made him pause. He looked at me and whispered softly, 'Relax, babe, I won't hurt you.'

I exhaled, then let go. I let go of everything including the condemnation I was feeling and allowed Sizwe to make love to me. The room was beyond warm, our bodies on fire. I held on tightly to him, digging my fingers into his back. With every movement, I discovered the addictive pleasures that come from that kind of pain. That night, Sizwe played and we sang a song of a different kind. It wasn't jazz. It was what I could describe as a classical piece of music that I would write about for the rest of my life.

* * *

Minnie's parents had been kind enough to drop me off at home after watching the show. Gospel music played softly in the background. I sat in the backseat looking out the window at the lights illuminating the streets of Johannesburg. I could still smell Sizwe's sweat on my body. I could still smell the scent of condoms on my hands. I could see him naked on top of me.

158

'You've always been a very quiet little girl, Naledi. Are you not shy when you have to act on stage?' Mamoruti asked.

I was in no mood for conversation and the most I could give her were 'yes' or 'no' answers. 'Naledi, are you okay?'

'Yes.'

'Are you not shy when you're acting on stage?' she asked again.

'No.'

'She must be tired – this school of theirs is very demanding,' Moruti added.

Moruti was right: I was extremely tired.

Mama was waiting for me at the gate. Her smile was broad as she watched me step out of Moruti's car. I hurried into the house, headed straight to the bathroom and left Mama to continue with small talk outside with Minnie's parents.

The first thing I saw when I took my clothes off was the blood on my underwear. I locked the bathroom door and ran a bath. I didn't want my grandmother walking in and busting me, analysing my bloodied panties. In the bath, I scrubbed my skin furiously like a person trying to get dirt out of a carpet. I needed to get the scent of sex and Sizwe off me. My mind was swimming. I wasn't sure how I would approach God moving forwards.

A banging on the door made me shoot out of the bathtub.

'Naledi, why is this door locked?'

I quickly grabbed the towel and drained the water.

'I'm almost done, Mama.'

'Since when do you lock the door when you bath? There are

159

no men living in this house and what exactly are you hiding that I haven't seen before?'

'Niks, I'm coming out now,' I said, scrubbing the bath clean with an old orange sack as we always did after bathing.

People say that once a woman has had sex, her body changed. That somehow you could tell by her walk, thighs and breasts that she was no longer a virgin. I stared at my body in the mirror while getting into my pyjamas. I turned around, bent over, touched and shook every part of me to see if my butt or thighs or breasts were by any chance sagging or wobbly. My breasts were still full and firm, and so were my thighs. Everything looked the same. It didn't change the fact that I was defiled.

* * *

'Unjani, Naledi,' Bra Joe rolled down his car window to greet me, driving past, making his way to his house. I gave him a wave and proceeded to sweep, watching the dust particles rise into the air with each brisk movement I made with the broom. I had become quite the pro.

Since the start of December, Bra Joe had driven past me every morning. Sis' Nozipho must have got tired of fighting the man because even though Bra Joe came home at six every morning, she never locked him out any more.

A vibration between my breasts interrupted my train of thought. My heart began to race. I stuck my hand down my T-shirt and into my bra. I couldn't mask my disappointment when I saw who was calling me.

'Friend, there's this hot guy I met in Fourways yesterday.

His name is Knox.' I could hear, through her voice, how broadly Minnie was smiling on the other end. I did a good job of pretending to be interested. But the only person I cared to hear from was Sizwe. Maybe there were so many street bashes happening in Gomorrah that he couldn't find the time to call me. Or maybe he had changed phones and lost my number. Maybe he had performances at end-of-year functions and weddings that were keeping him busy.

I sat in the kitchen staring at the plain white four walls for nearly half the day.

Mama was in the living room ironing while singing hymns to herself. Midway through a hymn, she put the iron down, with her one finger in the air and her head tilted up towards the ceiling. She allowed the hymn to transport her back to the pews of our church as she closed her eyes, her heavy vibrato sounding through her tenor: 'Yesu wena unguMhlobo, umhlobo womphefumulo, ndiza kuWe undincede, uncede le ntliziyo . . .'

Mama and I were in the same house but in two completely different worlds. I envied the rapture she was in. I'd rather be where she was than be sitting alone crying over a boy who was probably already having sex with another girl.

'Naledi, there is a church retreat I have to attend as one of the leaders ba ko kerekeng. Will you go to your mother for the weekend?' Mama said, walking into the kitchen.

'Why can't you ask MaKarabo if I can't stay there?' I asked.

'He, e Naledi, nnyaa. You want to go next door where you will be corrupted by that boy, no ways.'

I got up from the table. 'I am *not* going to Dineo,' I said. I

161

walked away from Mama and slammed the bedroom door shut. She swung the bedroom door open seconds later. By the time I turned my head, she was already standing in front of me. Her hand swept swiftly and strongly across my face. I caught myself on my way towards the floor, grabbing on to the bed to lift myself back up.

'Ke tlaa go bolaya ngwana Dineo! Who do you think you are, slamming doors in my house? Withhold not correction from the child: for if thou beatest him with the rod, he shall not die. Thou shalt beat him with the rod, and shalt deliver his soul from hell.'

She walked away and slammed the door behind her. I cried for a minute, trying to pull myself together. I was in shock that that had just happened – not the slap but how I had spoken to Mama, walked away and slammed the door.

I avoided her for the rest of the afternoon and figured that standing outside watching the people of Ndende Street pass by might do me some good. I hoped to see Lolo, but there was still no sign of him. I went back indoors when the sun went down. Mama went to bed without calling me in for prayers that night. Instead, I heard her casting out the spirit that was trying to take hold of me. A small part of me hoped that Mama's prayer would work, but instead I woke up with Sizwe still on my mind. I tried not to do anything that would further up-set my grandmother as we ate our porridge in the morning. After finishing our food without a word, Mama broke her silence.

'Naledi, if you are not scared to be by yourself, you can stay here.' Her anger towards me had subsided. It was even more comforting to know that I would be alone to clear my head for at least two nights.

*   *   *

Mama left the next afternoon. Fortunately, she had left without opening the post to check the mail which had my report card containing my exam marks. The impossible had happened – I, Naledi Kwena, had failed two subjects. I was devastated.

I was half-asleep on the couch when I heard the sound of the gate next door. I pulled the curtain to look out. Lolo was home.

He was surprised to see me. 'Magriza o kae? Isn't it way past your bedtime?' he teased.

I didn't find it funny. Instead, my eyes began to water.

'Mara, Lolo, why can't you be serious for once in your life?'

'No, askies, and I was being serious. I'm sorry, Naledi,' he said sincerely. 'But what if your grandmother catches you out here?'

'She's gone for the weekend,' I said.

Lolo paused and looked around us. 'My parents are sleeping in the house . . . We'll just chill in my room,' he said, taking my hand and leading me in.

I stepped into the yard next door. Neither of us wanted Lolo's parents to catch me sneaking into his backroom after midnight, so our footsteps were quiet and meticulous. Lolo closed the door softly. Once we got into his masculine-scented room, I kicked off my shoes then made myself comfortable on his bed. Lolo took off his sneakers, placing them with all the other sneakers and soccer boots that were neatly lined up against the wall. He removed his hoodie and placed it on a hanger inside his wardrobe. He came to sit next to me on the bed, and put his arm around me. Lolo knew that I needed to be held. With my head pressed against his chest, I told him that I had failed two subjects.

''Ska wara jo, it's varsity – everyone fails. And besides, you still get to do your second year next year so it's not a big deal,' he said.

Lolo had never been to university, so I didn't know how he knew all those facts. His saying that did sort of make me feel better, though it didn't eradicate my fear of what my grandmother would do once she got my results.

'If she can slap me for banging a door, Lolo, imagine what she's going to do when she sees this.'

'She slapped you, jo?' Lolo laughed.

'She slapped me so hard I was halfway to the floor before I realised what was going on – that's how dizzy I was.' Lolo's eyes filled with tears he was laughing so intensely as I explained the events to him. 'That night she hardly slept, she was busy casting out spirits and everything.'

'So your grandmother thinks you're possessed?'

'Not just me! Dineo too, even you, in fact Ndende Street kaofela!'

I was having such a good time humouring him that by the end of it we were both rolling on the bed drunk with laughter.

'Shh, shh, keep it down,' Lolo said.

Before I knew it, I found myself thinking about Sizwe again. If I didn't know any better, I'd be convinced that Sizwe had fed me korobela. A love potion would be the only reasonable explanation as to why I couldn't get through a single hour without the thought of him crossing my mind.

'Lolo, when a guy says to you that he wants to make you a woman, what does that mean?'

'What?' Lolo frowned. 'Who said that?'

'Just tell me, what does that mean?' I persisted.

'Did someone say that to you?'

Lolo insisted on getting the facts before finally answering me. I knew that Lolo's answer would hurt me; I had known the answer all along.

'Mxm, the guy just wants to smash. Whatever you do, don't go there with him,' Lolo said.

Self-pity, regret, sadness, guilt – a range of feelings came over me. Tears pooled in my eyes. Lolo immediately knew. I had already given up my virginity to a guy who cared nothing for me but instead had lied and deceived me just so that he could bruise me in the worst kind of way.

Lolo pulled me towards him. He kissed me on my forehead and on my cheeks. He apologised to me for what had happened, and for how it had left me feeling. It wasn't enough. I wanted more. I wanted Lolo to remove the pain that had lodged itself inside my chest. I wanted him to remove the shame that was seeping through my pores and dulling the glow of my skin. I wanted him to remove Sizwe's taste from my mouth. I grabbed Lolo's face and planted my lips on his.

He pulled back, placing his head between his knees. When he lifted his head, his eyes were red. We said nothing, only looked at each other in a way that we had never done before. He moved closer towards me and kissed me. When we came up for air, we both reached for our clothes and proceeded to take everything off. I had never seen a man with a body more perfect. He picked me up, with my legs wrapped around his waist. He pinned me against the wall and a second later I felt him enter me.

There wasn't a single scar on my body that Lolo did not see. There wasn't a place inside of me that I did not allow him to enter. Lolo had been holding on to a lot, too. We shared a common wound from the loss of Karabo. We had both lost our sounding board – though I knew for him the injury was greater. I surrendered completely and allowed him to use my body to release everything he had been carrying. When he was finished, he collapsed next to me. A few minutes later he moved closer, and clung to my body. I still felt empty. I could still see the loneliness he had been experiencing piercing through his eyes. We were left feeling shattered that we had failed to heal each other.

Motsamai o ja noha

*A traveller eats even a snake
on his journey*

Minnie found me in the middle of rehearsal and sat quietly in front of me, watching.

'I think you need to slow down a bit. Every word is important,' Minnie said when I was finished.

I had made it through the holidays without Mama and Dineo finding out that I had failed two of my theory subjects. But my failure gnawed at me.

I probably could have passed Sizwe's music theory exams with distinction; that's how much I had abandoned my own work to get absorbed in his.

When the first set of auditions for the term was announced, I was excited. If I got into this play, it would allow me to feel just a little bit absolved.

'Yes, you're right.'

'And be bigger, friend. I feel like you're holding back,' Minnie continued. 'And use your space. You have the whole stage to play with. Your face too.'

'Okay, friend, I get it!'

167

'Geez, don't get sensitive, Ledi. Every artist needs constructive criticism.'

'All right, thank you, Ms Anna, I do appreciate your *constructive criticism*,' I said sarcastically.

Itu arrived with Guitar Boy. They were each holding two coffees in their hands, one for each of us.

'So I got you all some good ol' caffeine to toast a new start to an awesome year ahead,' said Itu. She was wearing a bright African-print doek. No more of the colourful hair that we'd looked forward to seeing with the start of every new term.

'So is this like a standard requirement that once you've joined the SRC you have to start wearing doeks?' Guitar Boy teased.

Minnie and I laughed. I think we were both also wondering the same thing. At least she had kept her septum piercing and all the other rings on her body.

'The headwrap is the African woman's crown. White people came and stole almost everything from us and are still refusing to return our land back to us, but we still own our culture and our traditions. I've just taken a conscious decision to celebrate my blackness. You know, sort of like what Ledi does with her bantu knots,' Itu explained.

'I'm not trying to make any sort of statement with my hair, Itu. It's just an easy hairstyle that I've always done since I was a child,' I responded.

'It's an easy hairstyle that runs deep in the DNA of Southern African black women. It shows your history and your pride as a black girl, whether you are aware of it or not. Especially in

168

a world where wearing our hair like that has been regarded as ghetto, wild and unprofessional,' Itu continued.

'But why must we always reduce our display of pride as black women to what hairstyles we have?' Minnie added.

'It's not just hair, Minnie, even though hair is one way we use to express ourselves. It's our hair, our fashion, our language, history, culture and even our beliefs. All of it matters. It speaks to who we are and where we come from. The black woman is constantly degraded, abused, oppressed, killed and deemed the least valuable in the entire human race. It becomes that much more important for me to be loud and bold about being African, female and black,' Itu said passionately.

'Well, I think it's dope,' Guitar Boy said, staring longingly into Itu's eyes.

'*You* think a black girl is dope?' Itu smiled.

'What can I say, you've converted me.'

This was getting awkward. If Guitar Boy was truly developing feelings for Itu, he had better start learning to play some Thandiswa Mazwai songs fast because there was no quicker way to turn Itu off than to serenade her with some over-played American love songs.

'Here's to being black,' I said, raising my coffee cup in support of Itu's new stance and to get Itu and Guitar Boy to stop staring into each other's eyes like a pair of lovesick puppies.

The two girls and Guitar Boy raised their coffee cups with me.

'To being black!' they added.

'Wait, speaking of being black, what happened to your

Indian crush?' Minnie asked Guitar Boy. Clearly it wasn't just me who had noticed the cosiness between our two friends.

'Can we just focus on celebrating Itu's doek and leave irrelevant things alone,' said Guitar Boy.

'Oooooh!' The sting in Guitar Boy's statement was unmissable. We all burst out laughing. I guessed I wasn't the only one licking her wounds because of love.

Minnie thought that that moment would be the perfect time to propose her plans to us. These plans, however, did not include Guitar Boy, only Itu and me. I instantly knew that I would not like whatever she had up her sleeve.

'So the guy I'm seeing is having a little chillaz at his place and I think it would be the perfect time for my girls to meet him. Are you guys game to come to my house this weekend?' Minnie said excitedly.

'How are we gonna go out with Moruti and Mamoruti praying over us the entire day?' Itu asked, which I too felt was a valid question, as rude as Itu had been to say it.

'My parents won't be home Friday night. They'll be back Saturday afternoon,' Minnie assured us.

I really wasn't in the mood to spend yet another night out being bombarded with questions about my personal development. But I agreed anyway. I convinced myself that it would be better since the topic of my virginity was now off the table, even though I had yet to share this with my friends. I often saw Sizwe casually walking around campus and passing me by like my existence meant nothing to him. This was part of the reason why I couldn't bring myself to tell Itu and Minnie. It was embarrassing.

*　*　*

Friday after classes, with each of us carrying a weekend bag slung around our shoulders, we took the long walk down to the taxi rank together.

We arrived at Minnie's house, a modest four-bedroom double-storey in an estate where the people between middle class and rich lived.

'So this is where all the tithes and offerings go,' Itu remarked as we stepped through the big wooden door and into the all-white visitors' lounge.

Minnie led us up the stairs to her bedroom, ignoring Itu's comment. I must admit that seeing how big Minnie's bedroom was – it even came with its own bathroom – made me think of what Itu had just said. But then again, if we found our pastors' lifestyles offensive, we could always go to one of those churches that had services in a tent to which the pastor rode a bicycle wearing the same oversized suit every Sunday. Or we could worship Shembe, and have church out in an open field, and become one with nature in our white garbs. That thought alone made me thoroughly enjoy the hot water that skated along my body as I took a shower in Minnie's bathroom. Soon all three of us were dressed and ready to go.

Minnie stopped us as we were heading towards her bedroom door. She looked us up and down, me more than Itu.

'Ledi, don't you want to borrow my heels? I'm wearing heels and Itu's boots have a bit of a heel,' she suggested.

That question made me feel like I was sitting in an exam room writing a paper I hadn't studied for. I was going to fail this. What if I was one of those girls who transformed into a dinosaur when walking in heels?

'Look, friend, I'm comfortable like this.'

'Just try them,' she said, handing me two deadly weapons. Those shoes looked pretty high to me.

I wished Itu would speak up. Object to this madness. Throw in some feminist discourse about men creating high heels to objectify women and women having a right to choose if they want to learn how to walk in heels or not. But she just stood there scrolling through her phone, probably chatting to Guitar Boy.

I took the dreaded shoes, feeling both sad and terrified when I packed away my flats.

'One foot in front of the other and try to keep your legs straight,' Minnie coached me as I walked down the stairs.

* * *

It suddenly made sense why I was standing there in shoes that firstly weren't mine and secondly were killing me. Minnie's boyfriend had organised a cocktail party of about twenty people, not a 'chillaz' as Minnie had put it. When Minnie had said his name was Knox, I had expected someone our age and not a forty-year-old man.

Knox's friends were like him: they smelt good and drove

BMWs, Range Rovers and Mercedes-Benzes. They were dressed in crisp white shirts and had neatly trimmed beards. And they all moved through the room with an air of self-importance, whiskeys in their hands. I was reminded of Bheki, except that these gentlemen were slightly younger than him. There were other girls there too. The 'I only date a man who gives me money to do my hair and nails' Dineo-looking types who rocked long weaves and super-short dresses. Minnie fitted right in, showing off her ballerina body in a sexy white number.

I envied Itu's social skills, which she owed mainly to her book smarts.

'What exactly is the role of the EFF except to sit and criticise the corrupt ANC, as if they are a noble party themselves. And let's not even get started on the DA that has done nothing for the black people in Cape Town and yet wants to disguise racism by talking about a South Africa for all,' she said to a group of people.

That particular crowd was definitely to her liking. They spoke politics, race and more politics, which pulled Itu out of her initial shock and into comfortably sitting on the patio, beer in hand, debating up a storm.

I accepted the glass of wine that was offered to me by the bartender. It tasted far less bitter than the box wine that Itu and Minnie normally got drunk on. But as smooth as the wine was, it still wasn't pleasant on the palate. I just drank it because I knew that there was no way I was going to get through that night sober.

A guy came up to me and sat down in the chair next to

me. He introduced himself as Vuyani. I warmed up to Vuyani because he wasn't as old as the other male figures in the space. He was thirty-five, to be exact, and quite a pretty-faced type.

'I want to get something from the garage and also fill up with petrol – do you wanna come with?' he asked.

I hesitated. Minnie saw this and decided to agree on my behalf. 'Ledi's just shy,' she said, blowing cigarette smoke through her lips.

The drive was rather awkward. Just like the petrol tank, it was empty and silent. After filling up, we headed back to the cocktail party, or at least that's what I thought we were doing until I saw us parked outside a fancy apartment building not too far from Knox's place. Vuyani invited me in. I sat on the L-shaped couch inspecting the high ceiling and open-plan space, questioning how in the world I had found myself alone with a strange man who was sixteen years my senior. A chill shot through my back, knots formed in my stomach, and all I wanted to do was to take those damn shoes off!

'Would you like a drink?' he asked, pulling out a Sibongile Khumalo disk and placing it in his CD player.

He had great taste in design and music. 'Yes, please,' I said working very hard to give the guy a smile.

'I hope I'm not boring you with this music – I'm not much of a pop music type of a person,' he said, placing a drink in my hand before sitting down next to me.

It must have been my age that made him think that I was one of those Beyoncé or Drake fanatics. I couldn't really blame him.

'No, actually I really love jazz.'

That took him by surprise. He seemed to feel the need to test my knowledge.

'Oh, is that so? Then give me your top five.'

'My favourite guitarist is definitely Jimmy Dludlu. I love Andile Yenana on piano, and when it comes to vocals, without a doubt it's Mama Sibongile Khumalo, and I'm not just saying that because you're playing her music. But my favourite composer, singer, the king of the trumpet and jazz music in general, is—'

'Miles Davis,' he said, interrupting me.

I laughed. 'No, Bra Hugh,' I said.

'Oh, come on, you can't possibly choose Hugh Masekela over Miles Davis.'

'Well, a good friend of mine taught me always to celebrate my own first.'

The more we tossed back the red wine to the sounds of 'Yakhal' Inkomo' playing soothingly in the background, the easier our conversation flowed. There were no more awkward silences. I had kicked off Minnie's painful shoes and made myself comfortable on the couch. The distance between us grew smaller and smaller. It was Vuyani's words that speedily brought me back to reality.

'You're very beautiful, you know.'

That awkward silence resurfaced. Was that a question or a statement? Did it need a 'yes' or a 'no' answer?

Whatever Vuyani meant, I loved how it made me feel. I hadn't ever been described as 'beautiful' before. Sizwe had told me I was cute, not beautiful. It had been a long time since I had been able to look in the mirror and feel even a little bit pretty or worthy of any man's praise. This stranger looked at me and saw beauty, even with my cocoa skin, my hair twisted in knots and my thick waist.

Mafutsana a llelana

Orphans cry for each other

Where the heck was I? I turned my head and there he was. I lifted the white Egyptian cotton duvet cover. I was naked. He was naked. I counted breaths to calm myself. I began to recall the events that took place the night before.

One: I had been at a party with Itu and Minnie hosted by Minnie's boyfriend, Knox.

Two: The name of the stranger lying next to me was . . . Vu . . . ya . . . ni. Yes, Vuyani; he was one of Knox's friends.

Three: We had left everyone back at Knox's place, arrived at Vuyani's house and proceeded to drink wine.

Four: We had spoken mostly about music and then . . .

While I was still trying to remember what had happened after the last drink he had given me, his body began to move between the white covers. I remained very still. His eyes popped open. He raised his arm and flung it over my body.

'Hey,' he said and smiled.

His breath smelt of stale liquor. I remained quiet. He got on top of me. I turned my head to face the dull brownish wall.

His lips landed on my cheek. With my hand in a clenched fist I placed my arm between his torso and mine. Using my arm I tried to lift his body. He dropped his body lower.

His hand went down, tightly grabbed hold of my inner thigh and moved it to the side, parting my limbs. He pushed his pelvis hard between my legs, pressed hard again. Each thrust, a sharp jab into my taut abdominal muscles. I flinched. I flinched again and again each time he rammed himself into my cervix.

'Vuyani, get off me,' I finally said.

Vuyani continued.

'Vuyani, stop.'

I felt his weight pressing further down onto my body.

'Vuyani, please stop,' I pleaded this time.

Vuyani thrust harder.

He placed his hand on my chest, pinning me down to the bed and thrust faster. His groaning and breathing becoming heavier. Sweat dripped down onto my face. I turned to look at the sunrays beaming through the window. I focused on the warmth of the sun against my bare skin. I kept still and allowed him to finish.

He put on his briefs and disappeared into the bathroom. I felt lightheaded pulling myself off the bed. I found my scattered clothing and got dressed. Vuyani finally emerged from the bathroom, grabbed his car keys and walked out.

* * *

Minnie's ballerina feet had been so well trained that they could endure all kinds of torture. She lay stretched out on her bed with her white mini dress riding up her butt, still with her heels on. Itu was next to her, her 'African woman's crown' tossed to the floor. I couldn't sleep. My hands were trembling.

Knox had dropped us off at Minnie's house earlier. Before that, Vuyani had left me outside of Knox's house and sped off before I could open my mouth to say goodbye. I had heard the sound of his engine roaring with each gear change and acceleration two streets away. Sitting on the pavement barefoot, clutching Minnie's heels in my arms, I listened to the stillness that surrounded me on that quiet suburban street. After the fifth person had given me a strange look, I had figured I should wipe my tears and go inside before someone called the police on me.

The weight of my secrets was sitting heavily on my chest.

'I need to tell you guys about what really happened between Sizwe and me,' I said, sitting up on the bed.

Itu let her smart mouth get away from her.

'Ledi, we all know that you're not a virgin any more. Did you honestly think that Sizwe would keep that information to himself?'

Itu's words were like a ball being kicked at high velocity and landing directly on my face.

'I can't believe that you guys are talking about me behind my back instead of coming to me!' I yelled, scrambling to grab my toiletries. I had to leave – now!

'Whoa, wait, those rumours died down, friend . . .' Minnie was trying to calm the situation. 'And besides, I figured that you and Sizwe had done it because we had spoken about it, remember? Trust me, Ledi, nobody is talking about—'

I walked into the bathroom and slammed the door. The hot steam from the shower clouded the space. I wanted so badly to ascend into the air and then slip away.

Itu and Minnie kept knocking on the door, apologising for hurting me. I cried, even though I knew that they had nothing to do with my tears.

When I eventually mustered the courage to face my friends, I found them sitting on the bed with three glasses and two bottles of wine.

'I got it from Knox. It's the good stuff,' Minnie said.

I threw back the wine in a single gulp and stretched out my arm for a refill. The second glass slid down smoothly. The tension in my body was slowly peeling away.

'Sorry about what we said, friend,' Minnie said sweetly.

'Ja, chomi, askies,' Itu added.

'It's fine, guys . . .' I desperately wanted to talk about something else.

'So what happened? How was it? You said you wanted to tell us, so tell us.' Minnie was in interrogation mode.

On the tip of my tongue sat, *'It's none of your business'*, but I figured holding my tongue would be less offensive.

'I'm not sure if I want to hear about this. I'm a very visual person and I really don't want to be stuck with the image of Sizwe doing it in my mind,' Itu added.

'Come on, friend. Ignore this one. Deep down uyati naye that she also wants to know.'

I drank the last mouthful left in my glass. Hopefully this would be the last time I would have to talk about Sizwe.

'It was sore,' I said, shrugging.

I really didn't know where to start with such a conversation.

'So you regret it?' Itu asked.

I indicated I wanted another refill. Minnie complied but not without protest: 'Geez, Ledi, I've never seen you drink like this. Was it really that bad?'

'Just pour, Minnie,' I ordered.

Itu raised her glass. 'I have a strong suspicion that Sizwe is dead,' she said. 'The chapter of this douchebag is officially behind us. I say we have a toast.'

There were so many emotions moving through me that it was hard for me to raise my glass with the girls and cheers as if this were some sort of victory. I had gained nothing and lost everything. Losing Sizwe was a tough pill to swallow because my virginity and dignity had left with him.

I curled myself up into a ball on Minnie's bed and turned my head away. I wasn't sure what I was crying about: my heartbreak over Sizwe, or how I had not spoken to Lolo since that morning when he had snuck me out of his parents' yard, or the fact that I had been raped that very morning.

The girls were almost finished with the second bottle when we heard the gate opening and a car driving in. It was Minnie's parents. The girls downed the wine and shoved the bottles and glasses under the bed. I ran to the bathroom to splash water on my face. The girls came in to brush their teeth and we all threw chewing gum into our mouths.

We changed, sprayed an ocean of body spray on ourselves, then ran downstairs. Standing in a straight line like girls in assembly at a Catholic school, hands in front, straight backs and polite smiles, we waited to greet Minnie's parents.

'So how was your little slumber party?' Minnie's father asked, a kind smile on his face.

'It was very nice,' we said in unison.

We all played a good game of 'Who can act the most sober' while listening to Minnie's father go on and on about the lives he had seen being transformed through the ministry.

I kept looking at Itu. The super-short dashiki shirt dress she was wearing did a horrible job of hiding the multiple tattoos on her arms and the huge one that skated across her thigh and down to her calf. Minnie's mother seemed a little bit on edge, her piercing eyes sizing us up. Could she smell the alcohol? Could she tell that there was never a slumber party? Was the hangover and lack of sleep evident in our eyes?

It seemed Itu was too much for her. 'You know, there's a way in which a lady must carry herself so as not to bring across the wrong message. Actually, Itumeleng, when do you plan on coming to church? I have never seen you there,' Mamoruti said, adjusting her skirt to ensure that when she sat down it did not ride up to expose her knees.

Itu shifted in her seat. She leaned forwards and folded her arms. *Please don't say anything. Take a deep breath and stay calm. He's not just a pastor, he's Minnie's father and that's Minnie's mother and this is their house. That is a man and a woman of God, shepherds, disciples, leaders of our people.* I was saying all of this in my head but it was no good. Itu took the bait and went in for Mamoruti.

'Well, for me to come to church I would have to believe in a white man's Jesus. Which I don't.'

I knew that Minnie wanted to bury herself in the same hole I wished to be in.

'Askies?' Mamoruti was gobsmacked.

'Jesus came on the same three ships that got lost in the Cape and instead of carrying on on their merry way, those white men decided to point guns at our people and steal our land. They used that very story about Jesus to fool black people into believing that everything about us was vile and evil, from our skin colour to our ways of living, and even our beliefs. I'm not gonna go chasing after a foreign concept and deny the very things that have shaped my ancestry.'

I could tell by the expression on Minnie's mother's face that she was incensed and so was the pastor. Gone was his warm and friendly charm. Itu had not only insulted the pastor and his wife, but she had insulted Jesus, too.

Itu got up and I followed her upstairs to grab our stuff. When we came back down, Minnie was still sitting quietly looking at the floor.

'Bye, friend, and thank you so much, Moruti and Mamoruti,' I said, hoping they could feel my heartfelt apology through my words, and never tell my grandmother that I had befriended a heathen.

'Are you out of your natural mind?' I scolded Itu while we walked briskly to the taxis.

183

'No, I'm pissed off,' Itu responded.

'No, Itu, you're drunk. How can you talk like that to Minnie's parents?'

'Yeah, well, so what if I am drunk?' Itu stopped to face me. 'Does that suddenly give the world permission to berate me just because of my appearance? And what gives church people the right to undermine everyone else's beliefs, when no one must ever question theirs? That's bullshit, Naledi!'

*   *   *

I was staring at the ceiling in bed, Mama snoring and grinding her teeth next to me. Where were people like myself, Itu and Minnie meant to go to receive answers about our identity, sexuality, relationships and even God, if the church and our dinner tables did not permit such unsavoury talk?

When Mama woke me up the next morning, I felt like I had just closed my eyes.

'Yoh, Mama, I'm not feeling okay. My head hurts and I have stomach cramps,' I said, putting on my best act.

The thought of going to church was torturous. I wanted to lie in bed all day and feel miserable. Mama sat beside me on the bed. She put one arm around me and placed her other hand on my forehead.

'Rra Rra, you alone understand what is going on in Naledi's body but we speak your healing over her life. Whatever sickness she may have, we tell it to leave her body immediately. This we ask in your name, Amen.'

When Mama finished praying over me, she got up and

184

walked away. A victory dance began inside me, but my celebration was short-lived because as Mama reached the bedroom door, she turned to me:

'For we wrestle not against flesh and blood, but against principalities, against powers, against the rulers of the darkness of this world, against spiritual wickedness in high places. Wherefore take unto you the whole armour of God, that ye may be able to withstand in the evil day, and having done all, to stand. These things, Naledi, you shouldn't take them lightly. These are attacks from the devil. But as God's children, we have power and victory. Get up and you'll see that you are well; I'll go pour water for you in the bath while you make the bed.'

I threw myself back down, defeated. Nothing could get past this woman! I mustered the strength to get up, make the bed, take a bath, and get dressed in my Sunday best before joining my grandmother for breakfast in the kitchen.

'You see the tricks that the devil comes up with? Why would you get sick on a Sunday of all days when you've been fine the whole week?' Mama said, contentedly eating spoonfuls of brown porridge. What Mama failed to realise was that I was the 'devil' that she kept referring to, who was manufacturing tricks to get me out of having to go to church.

* * *

Mama taught an early morning class to the new church members. But even though it felt like the crack of dawn, Minnie was already there waiting for me inside the main church building.

'So what did your parents say?' I asked.

'Blessed is the man who walks not in the counsel of the ungodly . . .' she said, imitating an American Baptist preacher in a pulpit.

I joined her to finish it: 'Nor stands in the way of sinners, nor sits in the seat of the scornful.' We laughed ourselves silly.

'Yeah, friend, so you know very well the sermon that I got, I don't have to tell you. But it only lasted for about two hours, followed by an hour of them praying over me; you know, nothing too hectic,' Minnie said sarcastically. 'I could do with a cigarette right about now.'

'Haa, Minnie, at church?'

'Oh, so you of all people are judging me?'

'No, I would never judge you, friend, but—'

'Okay then, let's go,' Minnie insisted.

I followed Minnie to a hidden spot tucked between an old storage room and some large rocks on the church grounds.

'Relax, Ledi, no one comes this side. I know every corner of this church, so chill. And besides, smoking is not the worst thing I've done here.' Minnie giggled, taking a long drag of her cigarette. Then she let out why she'd brought me there: 'So friend, what happened with you and Vuyani?'

I felt my chest tightening and my breathing quickening at the mere mention of his name.

'Geez, Minnie, nothing!'

'Okay, well, if it's nothing, why are you being so touchy?'

I didn't respond to Minnie's question, which made her probe even further.

'I'm only saying this because he told Knox that he smashed you.'

'What the hell is wrong with these guys? Sies, maan!'

I walked away. Minnie put out her cigarette and ran behind me.

'Guys are stupid,' she said, grabbing my hand. I turned to face her. 'They are just dumb losers who always feel the need to brag about getting laid. Look, Ledi, it's chilled, all right. Don't be so hard on yourself.'

I lowered my head, fighting to hold back my tears. Minnie could see my glistening eyes and pulled me to sit on the rocks.

'Minnie, can you get me the pill?' I passed the question through my lips with so much difficulty, it shot a sharp pain to the centre of my chest.

Minnie didn't pause to think about her answer. 'Don't stress, I got you, friend. I'll go buy it for you and show you exactly how to take it. I'll have it tomorrow morning by the time you get to campus.'

She told me the scandalous story of what she had done with one of the youth leaders right there behind the old storage room.

'A lot happens at church, Ledi. A lot.' Minnie giggled like a mischievous high-school girl. 'I guess I figured very early into the game that a girl must never allow herself to fall too hard. You must never love a guy more than he loves you. It needs to be the other way around, otherwise a guy will always make an ass out of you.'

Minnie possessed a level of control over guys that I envied. How she could manage her emotions like that was incredible to me.

Midway through the service, Minnie and I snuck in after spraying deodorant on ourselves to kill the smell of her cigarette. Most people were too caught up in the spirit to even notice us. The passion that these people had for the Lord was unmistakable. Tongues poured out of their mouths like gushing waters. Streams of tears swept down their faces as they prayed with their hands raised to the heavens. Some seemed to be slain by the spirit, dropping down on the floor in front of the altar. In all the years that I had been in the church and in all the times that Moruti had laid his hands on me, I had yet to fall and have the ushers fan me to help me gain control of myself.

Minnie handed me a piece of paper.

'When I go up, you're gonna come up with me,' she whispered. 'You'll read the announcements, then I'll do the closing prayer.'

It was a horrible idea. Before I could refuse, Minnie was on her way to the pulpit. I walked slowly towards the microphone. I hoped that people couldn't see that my hands were shaking. I looked around the room and saw Mama. Mama sat up in her seat. I had never seen such pride on her face before. I read with as much poise as I could muster. Minnie closed off the service with what Mama later on described as a 'powerful prayer'. Deep down I knew that God couldn't have been pleased.

Ingwe idla ngamabala

A leopard eats by means of its spots

Typical of a morning in mid-July, the sun made its way weakly through the overcast sky, its heat swallowed by the winter chill. A long line of people waiting to buy their Saturday morning magwinya started outside the Somalian man's shop and ran into the small vetkoek-and-snoek haven.

Lolo and a group of his friends from our area were huddled by the corner of the shop. I hadn't spoken to Lolo in months, which came as no surprise after what had happened between us. He had sneaked me out of his room at the crack of dawn before MaKarabo woke up to go sweep. We had looked at each other captured by the uneasy air that had stood between us. Then he had reached out to hug me. Something about it had felt forced.

I had learned the hard way that sex turned even the most seemingly honest men into liars. I had still felt compelled to ask him anyway, even though I had known he would lie.

'Lolo, are we still friends?'

'Uh jo, you can never get rid of me!'

189

And that was the last thing he had said to me in over six months.

I needed to find a way to get out of that Somalian man's shop without Lolo seeing me. I clutched the bread under my arm, pulled my hoodie over my head and walked quickly, trying to hide myself behind the line of people in the queue. As soon as I crossed the street, from behind me, I heard 'Naledi, Naledi, wait!'

Damnit!

I stopped, pulled my hoodie down and waited for him to make his way across to me.

'Did you not see me standing over there?' he asked.

'No, I didn't, askies.'

Lolo was all cool and nonchalant. 'Yoh jo, so I got picked to play for a professional club, mfethu. Some very important people who came to the tournament the other day saw me doing my thing, and now I'm in.'

I jumped into his arms and wrapped my legs around his waist, with his arms tightly holding on to me as I screamed in elation.

'I've been training, doing camp – you know, the whole thing. Eh rea vaya, Naledi, we are heading for the big leagues,' he said with much bravado.

I immediately felt stupid for trying to avoid him earlier.

'Ne ke na le stalker jo. I had to change my number to get away from this crazy chick,' Lolo said in his not-so-serious way of talking about serious things, giving me his new cell-phone number. Lolo stopped to look at me. 'Keng o sharp?'

190

I assured him that I was just tired. He asked me about my mother and I simply shrugged. 'Psssh, I don't know where Dineo is. Still happily living her life, I guess.'

I was relieved when Thabiso seemingly sprang out of nowhere and interrupted us.

'Sho, bafwethu,' he greeted us, then asked for two rand.

People who had a habit of asking for money seemed to always ask for two rand.

'Hade, mfethu, I don't have,' Lolo said, hitting the sides of his pockets to show Thabiso that there were no coins in there.

I had bread in my hands and some change. Thabiso looked at me. 'Uh, my sister . . .' He placed his one palm on top of the other, to emphasise his humbling himself. 'Ngiyacela, my sista, please, my sista.' He rubbed his belly to show me that he was hungry too.

Thabiso had certainly changed a lot from being that guy that hung out beneath the tree with Clement. He looked older. With his brown teeth, dirty clothes and scrawny frame, I wondered if he remembered who I was. Could he still remember that I was that girl he used to make feel uncomfortable whenever he threw lewd comments at me about my butt, or had nyaope eaten away more than his looks?

'I was sent to buy bread; it's not my money,' I explained to him.

Without another second wasted, he dashed off to the next person.

I embraced Lolo, holding on to him a little longer than usual.

'Yoh, you've really missed me, neh?' he teased.

'Who knows, maybe,' I said, and smiled.

*   *   *

I arrived bright and early before most students for class. The cast list for Professor Addington's rendition of *Sophiatown* was already up on the notice board and my name was on it. Without formally discussing it, the three of us had set our sights on making a mark by the end of the year. Itu was aiming to get her work in the university's art exhibition and Minnie, unlike Itu and me, had long cemented her role as the lead in the ballet. Itu and I had resorted to spending our breaks in the ballet hall because that was the only way we could have time with Minnie.

'You're starting to look really skinny, you know that?' Itu said devouring a burger.

'I'm a ballerina, Itu, I can't be fat. Already my ass is bigger than every other ballet dancer's in the class.'

'You might be a ballerina, but you're also a black girl – you can't compare yourself to the white girls in your class. Ass is in our DNA. Go anywhere else in the world, women are inject-ing things into themselves just to have a big bum. We were handed big bums on a silver platter. There are not a lot of things that have just been handed to us, so be grateful.'

Minnie, who talked between doing pirouettes and allegros, frowned at Itu. 'How many times must I tell you that eating is not allowed.'

'Chill, I won't make a mess,' Itu brushed off Minnie's remarks before jumping back to the previous topic. 'I mean I don't know many skinny Swati chicks. Actually, Nguni people as a whole have meat on their bones. And the men like their women with a little something they can grab and keep warm with.'

'Since when do you care about what men like?' I asked Itu suspiciously.

Minnie stopped twirling for a second and came to sit down on the floor with us.

'And not only that, I thought Itu was all about not classing and objectifying women. What happened to my feminist of a friend?' Minnie added.

'Look, I'm not objectifying women, I'm just stating the facts. Everyone knows that Nguni men like big women' Itu said.

'Damn, I never thought I'd see the day that Itu would be stereotyping people,' I teased.

'Okay, let me prove my point.' Itu put down her burger, licked her fingers and wiped her hands with a serviette. She got to her feet. 'Ledi, you are a thick girl, right, and let's look at the guys who've shown interest in you: Sizwe – Zulu, Vu-yani – Xhosa, and what's that high-school boy's name who got your friend pregnant?'

At the mention of Sizwe's name, my palate went dry. When she said 'Vuyani', my stomach turned. At this point, high-school matters were completely irrelevant . . .

'Sihle!' Minnie shouted out, laughing. 'And he's one of the Ngunis for sure.'

'My point exactly. And look at Minnie – because she has

193

that ballet stick-figure body, Pedis and Sothos and Tswanas and the rest of them swarm around her.'

Minnie had collapsed onto the floor and wrapped her arms around her belly, she was laughing so hard.

'I thought Knox was Zulu,' I said.

'Actually, Knox speaks Zulu because his mom is Zulu; his dad is Pedi,' Minnie explained. 'And for the record, Itu, there are plenty of Nguni guys who love my body and it is *not* a stick-figure body, okay,' Minnie said, pulling herself back up to a sitting position.

'Fine, just remember to slow down a bit. Give your body a break,' Itu advised.

I wasn't sure if Minnie knew what *slowing down* meant or what *giving her body a break* entailed. Things had come to an ugly end between her and Knox because even though Minnie loved boys, boys were no match for ballet.

'I doubt Kitty Phetla got to be where she is by slowing down. And anyway, to get into Juilliard, I need to be the best; there's no time for sitting on my bum and eating burgers.' Minnie stood up. 'I need to work, it's time for you two to leave.' She snapped her fingers and pointed to the door.

* * *

I was rushing to be early for my first rehearsal after classes when, like a hyena, Sizwe appeared and snatched my joy.

I wanted to turn and walk the other way but that would have been too obvious. Sizwe and I had found a way to act like we were invisible to each other. This face-to-face, eyeball-to-

194

eyeball encounter with no one else around us would be the first in a very long time.

'Unjani, Ledi?' he greeted me.

I didn't greet him back. Instead, I glared at him, masking my inner turmoil with an attitude.

'I've been wanting to talk to you. Grand sharp, I wanted to apologise for what happened. I'm not that kind of a cold-hearted bastard and it's been eating me up inside the way I treated you,' he said.

I walked away without giving him a response. Sizwe kept calling after me: 'Ledi . . . Ledi . . . Naledi!'

I didn't look back. After walking for a distance I turned around and saw that he was gone. I then ran to the girls' bathroom and locked myself in one of the cubicles. I cried out silently, before collapsing on the floor.

Mosadi o tshwara thipa
ka mo bogaleng

A woman holds a knife
at its sharpest end

Saturday morning while polishing the stoep I heard the clicking of heels moving closer towards me. I turned around. She
was dragging a big suitcase and carrying another smaller bag.

'I'm just going to put these here and get the rest from the
van,' a man said, coming from around the corner holding two
more big boxes.

'Ea, I'm back,' Dineo said, probably noticing the confusion
on my face.

Her thick makeup couldn't hide the dark rings around her
eyes. She looked at me and I looked at her, both of us taciturn.
I could feel that she wanted to hug me and apologise but I was
glad that she didn't try to.

'Mama,' I called out. 'M-a-m-a!'

'Naledi, keng?' Mama ran out with a doek wrapped loosely
around her head and a broom in her hand. She paused for a
second, looking at all the boxes and bags that were placed
around Dineo and me. 'Are you back?' she asked sharply.

Dineo said nothing, only nodded.

The tension was interrupted by the man bringing in the last few boxes. 'Ja, that's everything,' he said. Seeing my grandmother, the man quickly took off his hat, clutching it in his hands before giving a slight nod. 'Dumela, mama,' he said, before putting his hat back on.

Mama gave a slight wave. 'Ea rra.'

Dineo thanked the man and he left after she handed him money.

'Just make sure that you unpack all these things. I don't want those boxes cluttering my house,' Mama said, heading back to finish sweeping inside the house.

Dineo unpacked for most of the day, while I finished my chores before sitting down to watch television. The weather changed suddenly. A gust of wind began to blow. Clouds darkened the Pimville area and after a few minutes the rains fell heavily with thunder.

'Naledi, lightning!' Mama shouted from the bedroom.

I got up to unplug all the electrical appliances. Mama believed that if any electrical appliance was used or switched on during a thunderstorm, lightning would strike and possibly set fire to the house. I had an unsettled feeling in my stomach and didn't want to be alone, so I went to the bedroom. Mama told me to cover the mirror using the big towel, which I did before sitting on the bed.

The room felt tight, smaller than usual with all three of us and Dineo's clothes scattered on the floor. We listened to the thunder, while Dineo continued to pack away her clothing. My mind was loaded with a thousand questions and my anxiety was getting the best of me. To distract myself, I helped Dineo unpack. There were bags, shoes, jeans, dresses, skirts, and a plethora of makeup. Some of the stuff couldn't fit into the space Mama had provided.

'Owa ma, did all you and that devil do was shop? Is that what kept you there, clothes and handbags?' Mama asked in an offhand manner, breaking the silence.

Dineo didn't respond and once again the tension mounted through a thick air of unspoken words. The thunder roared and crackled in and over the roof. I cowered, dropping the skirt that I was folding onto the floor.

God was angry.

Mama began to pray, asking God to pardon us. This was the one time when Mama prayed with her eyes open. 'Forgive us, Lord, for our transgressions. Have mercy on us. Don't take us yet,' she prayed with her eyes fixed on Dineo.

I hoped that she would keep her focus on Dineo and not look in my direction and see my nerves.

'Some of these things will have to stay in boxes; there's no more space,' Dineo said, adding the last item that she could squeeze into the cupboard and closing it.

Mama sat on the bed still praying. She had yet to take her eyes off my mother. She followed her around the room, watching Dineo pack and sort the rest of her belongings back into boxes. The storm eased outside and Mama thanked God for His mercy before saying Amen.

'Who got tired of who?'

Mama's question brought a sudden stillness to everything

within the walls of our house. I looked at Dineo. Her eyes were also now on her mother.

Mama asked again, 'Who got tired of who, Dineo?'

Dineo remained tight lipped, her eyes changing form and colour.

Mama continued: 'Before you can attempt to layer bricks, a foundation must be set. Look at this house that was built by your father – years have come and gone and yet it still stands. It is kept by my prayers. That is the foundation ya ha mo-Kwena. You began to build a home and now the walls have come down because not only did you leave this house without the blessing of your father, but you cursed his name with your own mouth. You built a home without God, thinking that the things of this world were worth more. Today you are left standing organising the remains of your marriage into boxes. A marriage that began with you tearing down the walls of another woman's home and then you young girls wonder why things fall apart.'

It must have been from the guilt I carried concerning my own transgressions that I felt rebuked sitting there.

I turned to look at Dineo. Her face was glossed in tears. I could see it again – her yearning to say, *I'm sorry*. I wanted to embrace her this time but I just couldn't move.

* * *

Having Dineo back was different. Mama was critical about everything that she did.

'Did you soak these clothes before washing them? Have you

199

now got so used to fancy washing machines that you cannot wash clothes properly any more?' Mama said, hovering over her shoulder while Dineo was bent over the bathtub.

'A woman doesn't wait for the sun to burn her sheets before getting up. The yard must be swept before your husband and children wake up!' Mama spoke at the very top of her voice yanking the blankets off Dineo in the living room at five.

While Dineo swept, Mama would walk to the window every now and again to check if she was doing it correctly.

Dineo walked into the house sneezing. 'Mama *(achoo)*, I've got *(achoo)* sinuses, I can't *(achoo)*,' she said, a sneeze punctuating every word.

'Dineo, go and sweep, maan! Don't tell me about sinus. Must the world now stand still because Dineo is sneezing? Sinus, ya nonsense!' Mama yelled.

Dineo, defeated by Mama, walked back out with almost the entire roll of toilet paper tucked into her bra. She sneezed and swept. She blew her nose, then stopped to wipe the sweat splatters on her forehead, then swept. People walked past and looked at her with gossip hovering over their lips. Felicia slowly stepped towards our gate. I stood at the window watching them, waiting to see how this battle between the old foes would end.

'Helang basali.' Felicia laughed, mockingly raising her voice so that everyone in our street could hear her. 'Ebile orwetse tuku, heeeee che mohlolo. I heard people saying that you were dragging boxes and suitcases, keng sistas, o hlolehile lenyalong? So you've run back to suck your mother's breast, huh?'

200

Felicia walked away still antagonising Dineo, talking loudly over to the neighbours, 'There she is holding a broom and sweeping with a headwrap around her head wearing a pinafore, still posing as a married woman!'

I had thought that Dineo would attempt to strike Felicia with the broom or simply cuss her out. To Felicia and my surprise, though, Dineo just scoffed and continued to sweep.

* * *

It had been a while since it was just the two of us. Mama left me alone with Dineo to go attend another one of her church retreats. We sat down to eat in the kitchen and all you could hear was our chewing and the sounds of our spoons hitting against our plates. The awkwardness was elevated by Dineo's peculiar question.

'Have I been gone that long, Naledi?' she said. I remained quiet. 'Something is not right with you and I know I'm not the most maternal woman in the world but I'm still your mother and I can tell that I've missed something.'

I continued to eat my cabbage and pap as if I were indulging in ribs, ignoring my mother.

Someone was playing loud music from his car out in the streets but even that failed to dilute the brewing tension in the kitchen.

'Naledi, you're angry about something. I can tell,' Dineo continued. 'Just say what you need to say. Trust me, I can take it.'

I got up and cleared the table. I scraped the pots and moved

201

the plates and spoons about in the kitchen, not trying to hide my irritation. Dineo stormed out. Moments later a loud *vroom, vroom, vroom* roared through Ndende Street and Dineo was gone.

* * *

The house looked nothing like how I had left it before going to bed. I wasn't surprised to see the mess after hearing the drunken noise Dineo and her friends were making at two o'clock when they brought her back. She lay passed out on the living room floor. I wanted to grab her by her expensive weave and drag her out of my grandmother's house.

I went to fill a bucket with cold water, grabbed a mop, then went back into the living room.

Dineo snored, allowing her boozy breath to fill the stuffy room. I leaned the mop against the wall and dropped the cold water from the bucket onto her body. Dineo screamed, 'Aaaaahhhh, Naledi!'

She sprang to her feet, her eyes wide open, soaking wet.

'Oh my word, I'm so sorry. I tripped and the bucket just flew out of my hands,' I said.

My pleasure quickly died down when I had to go out to sweep, polish the stoep and windowsills, then come in to clean the house and to do the laundry while Dineo slept on my grandmother's bed for half the day nursing her hangover. Over dinner, she made another attempt at creating conversation.

'You did stay okay by yourself last night?'

I couldn't catch my tongue in time to stop my venom from spewing out.

'What do you think? Mxm!'

I got up from the table in a bolt of fury. Dineo followed behind me; 'Don't say "mxm", Naledi! You forget that I'm your mother. You can't just talk to me in any which way that you please,' Dineo barked.

'Oho, you are about as useful as that thing called Xolani. What's even more disgraceful is the fact that I have seen more of his face than I've seen of you over the last few years. Don't come and call yourself a mother. Whose mother, yeh? Mme wa mang Dineo?'

Dineo sat down on the couch, quietly quivering. Tears poured down her rosy cheeks. I went outside and sat in the dark behind the outdoor toilet. The stars were unusually bright, covering the vastness of the midnight-blue sky. It looked like I was somewhere else far away in a remote village and not in a loud township breathing heavily and feeling my heart pounding in my chest. I looked at the small rocks where I hid my journal, but I didn't get it out. I knew it wouldn't help me any more.

There had always been someone in my life with whom I could share my injuries, whether it was Karabo, Sindi, Itu, Minnie or Lolo, but not this time. Not with something like this. As if someone had violently ripped my tongue out of my mouth, Vuyani's assault had silenced me.

Ri de ndi mbidi ro vhona mavhula

*We will say it's a Zebra
after seeing the stripes*

My birthday was only a few days away. Dineo found a single hundred-rand note and counted the last cents in her purse and handed them to me.

'I want you to look beautiful for your birthday. Nozipho must relax your hair and re-do it nicely the way you like it,' she said.

Sis' Nozipho was excited to see me as always. 'Yazi, you are one of my favourite customers, Naledi,' she said, before turning to brag to all the other ladies in the salon: 'I've been doing her hair since she was a little girl and you'll see now how long it is when I undo it.'

That's who I was: *Umnyamane with the bantu knots*.

Sis' Nozipho untwisted each one of my knots and my hair flowed down elegantly past my shoulders. My hair had even grown longer than Minnie's hair. The women in the salon watched in awe like children filled with wonder at a magic show. They no longer saw the darkness of my skin and the fullness of my thighs that they had seen when I first walked in.

It was only about the beauty of my crown that had been faithfully worked on by Sis' Nozipho's hands for many years.

Sis' Nozipho reached for the Dark and Lovely box. 'Are we just relaxing your hair today, sthandwa sami?' she asked.

'No, I'm not. I'm cutting it,' I said.

Sis' Nozipho froze. Gugu, who was busy with another client's hair, turned to look at me like I had just uttered profanities at her.

'What do you mean, cutting?' Sis' Nozipho asked. 'Do you mean the split ends?'

'Cut it all off,' I said.

Sis' Nozipho spent the next twenty minutes trying to talk me off the cliff. Gugu joined in, the two sisters circling my chair to stage an emergency intervention.

'Cut it and leave nothing,' I said, putting an end to the discussion.

The blade ran through my long hair and slowly my scalp began to appear like the crowning head of a newborn baby. I left the salon with the sun beating against my bald shiny head. I had barely taken two steps into the house when Dineo shouted, 'You cut your hair!'

'Yerrr, you look exactly like that drunk,' Mama shot out, triggering Dineo.

Dineo stormed out of the kitchen. I headed for the bathroom. I needed to shut the world out for just a moment. While waiting for the water to fill the bathtub, I stood naked, staring into the mirror. Xolani's face was staring back at me. Smooth cocoa-brown skin, slightly boyish, with my forehead looking more pronounced. I certainly could no longer distract people with the cuteness offered to me by my youthful girly knots. My big brown eyes betrayed me, displaying every emotion I had tucked away. The veil was gone.

*　*　*

Lolo knew all too well that parties were not my scene. I had explained this to him a number of times already. He had concluded that it was because I had never been out with him before. He called me 'stiff' and blamed that on being raised by my grandmother. His exact words went something like, 'Wena jo, you are what white people call an old soul.' And how Lolo would remedy this would be by taking me out clubbing for the first time as my birthday present. When I shared this with Itu, Minnie and Guitar Boy, to my dismay they all agreed with him and supported the notion of entering my twenties by breaking my club virginity.

'It's about damn time,' Minnie said.

Apparently varsity bashes and house parties didn't count as clubbing.

Mama was always thrilled whenever I indicated that I would be sleeping over in the house that prays. She imagined our weekends at Minnie's house to be filled with Saturday mornings where we would be walking the streets evangelising and afternoons taking prayers to the sick people in hospitals. The truth was that I would be sneaking into Minnie's residence on that Friday and Minnie and I would only be heading to her parents' house on Saturday afternoon because of our 'hectic rehearsal schedules'. This was to ensure that when Sunday came, we'd both be in church fulfilling our duties. I had a new promotion at church. My record church attendance and my 'good English', combined with how well I performed in front of an audience, had landed me the enviable permanent position of announcement girl. Packing my clothes into my weekend bag, I made peace with the guilt I knew I would feel come Sunday morning after I had committed all the transgressions which awaited me that Friday night.

* * *

As soon as my rehearsals ended, I grabbed my bags and went to the art department to look for Itu. Guitar Boy sat on top of a desk watching Itu who stood in front of her canvas with a paint brush in her hand.

'Hey, Ledi,' Guitar Boy said, tying his long thick dreadlocks into a top-knot.

'Hey, Guitar Boy,' I said, hoisting myself up onto the table next to his.

Without turning around to face me, Itu barked, 'That's not his name, Naledi!'

The look on Guitar Boy's face was the same expression I had on mine. We both didn't know where that had come from.

Itu threw her paint brushes into her toolbox and went to mount her incomplete painting with the other paintings on the opposite side of the room. Guitar Boy and I remained quiet, following Itu with our eyes. Clearly Itu was in one of her moods and I was the last person who wanted to start an argument with her. We grabbed our bags, with Guitar Boy offering to carry my heavy weekend bag for me, and headed towards the main theatre.

'I'll catch you guys tonight at the club,' Guitar Boy said, handing me my big bag.

'Thanks, we'll see you later Guita—' I caught myself before finishing my sentence. I turned to look at Itu, who was shaking her head and rolling her eyes at me.

'Do you like it when Xolani calls you "Mnyamane"?'

'Babe, it's not that deep,' Guitar Boy quickly jumped in, seeing where Itu was going with that question.

'No, why must they call you that?' Itu said, before turning her attention back to me. 'It's not nice when people do it to you, so you and Minnie need to drop this 'Guitar Boy' shit!'

I was taken aback, but not by Itu's outburst and sudden amnesia, since she had also always called Lwandle that; I was taken aback by Guitar Boy calling Itu 'babe'.

'Sorry, Lwandle, I didn't mean to hurt your feelings,' I said.

'I've never taken any offence – you really don't need to apologise,' Guitar Boy said.

'Yes, she does need to apologise,' said Itu.

For the sake of peace, I was going to drop the whole Guitar Boy thing and I hoped Minnie would do the same and not fight Itu on this one. I wasn't so sure if I would be able to drop the 'babe' thing, though.

Ms Anna was drilling Minnie like a military sergeant in the theatre. Minnie looked phenomenal to me. Every jump, every stride, every arch and every turn looked like perfection. Ms Anna was even more impressive than Minnie, though, possessing the ability to turn and lift her leg effortlessly, unlike any woman I had seen who was way into her fifties.

'You do know that if Minnie weren't black, she wouldn't be this hard on her,' Itu said as we watched Minnie from upstairs in the gallery. 'Especially if she wants to dance against the best in the world, as a black girl she must work harder.'

'Itu, it's not like that any more. There are plenty of black ballet dancers now. Ms Anna is a fine example of that,' I said.

'Ledi, don't be naïve. We live in a world where big asses and small waists buy women success, popularity and beauty titles. Our industries are run by predators where a whole president can be accused of rape and still occupy office and have other women, who are supposed to be our mothers and leaders, defend and protect him. And you think with your dark skin and bald head that you won't have to fight?'

Itu had described her mother to us as a comrade who had strapped Itu on her back as a baby to attend rallies. The result of this was raising a daughter who had developed an appetite for umzabalazo, with her sights set on becoming the Frances Baard or Winnie Mandela of our generation. Today, I wasn't in the mood for one of Itu's lectures, though. She hadn't even said happy birthday to me. I just wanted Minnie to finish so that I could enjoy what was left of this day.

The two of them had bought me a dress as a gift. This, I knew, was the only way they could get me to wear something that was a little more club appropriate. That was my first

209

transgression of the night. I was breaking not only the laws of the church, but also the unspoken rules of society: chubby girls were not allowed to wear short tight dresses and feel that good about it.

Lolo's eyes widened and his jaw dropped when he saw me. He had arrived to pick us up, travelling with one of his soccer buddy friends who immediately took a liking to Minnie.

'So when exactly did Mme Norah start buying you minis?'

Itu joined in on Lolo's banter: 'Careful now, chomi, one too many short dresses, you might just fall short of the pearly gates.'

Who else but true friends could introduce a girl to the power of the little black dress.

*   *   *

The club experience was rather uncomfortable. I didn't understand how someone you didn't even know could just start grinding up against you while you tried to dance, or spill beer all over you. Better yet, how random fights between two guys would break out over some girl they had just spotted and had barely said two words to.

'Just blunt, drink and dance, then all these things will fade away, I promise.'

Those were Lolo's words of wisdom, giving me a lesson on 'How to handle your first experience in a club 101'.

Lolo and I sat in a corner outside where a number of people were smoking cigarettes, hookah and dope. Lolo crushed and rolled the joint as if there were some kind of a science to it.

He measured and folded the Rizla, and then meticulously lined the dope along its clear fabric with great focus and precision.

'You're quite the expert, aren't you?'

'I've been naughty for a long time, Naledi,' he said, lighting up the joint, before taking a drag and then passing it to me.

As I breathed in, the smoke engulfed my throat. My chest was on fire. I coughed bitterly and the only thing Lolo could do was laugh.

'Are you okay, Naledi?' he asked, still chuckling.

'I think so,' I said, struggling through the cough while fighting to catch my breath.

Once Lolo was finished amusing himself, he explained that the coughing was a good sign because it meant that I would get high. I didn't feel high.

Lolo grabbed my hand and dragged me back inside, pulling me towards the bar. 'Two shots of tequila, a glass of red wine and a beer, please.'

'Coming right up,' said the cute white bartender.

I looked out to my left, and Minnie and Itu were both coupled up. Itu and Lwandle were sitting in a corner with Lwandle's arm wrapped around Itu's shoulder, while Minnie danced very seductively in front of Lolo's friend, who stood gaping at her with a drink in his hand. I decided it was safer to stare straight ahead.

'Here you go,' Lolo said, placing the tequila and wine in front of me. 'On three, we down it. Ready?' I nodded slowly. 'One . . . two . . . three . . .'

I quickly grabbed the wine to wash down the fiery taste that shot through my mouth from the tequila.

'Want another one?' Lolo offered with a smirk on his face.

I took him by the hand and pulled him away from the bar, attempting to take his mind off getting me wasted. Our bodies moved to the loud music played by the DJ on the dance floor. We went hard and fast at times, but in moments the collision of our rhythm was smooth and sensual. I began to sweat and so did he. I was lost for a while, free from all inhibitions.

Our tight little spot in the corner was still vacant when we went back outside. Lolo glanced at me and smiled.

'Girls usually look weird ka chiskop, but shockingly this doesn't make you look like a guy. Nkare o Zikhona Sodlaka,' he said.

'I think I look like a boy.'

'Zikhona doesn't look like a boy.'

'So comparing me to Zikhona Sodlaka is your way of telling me that you think I'm beautiful? Why don't you just say it?'

I had definitely got the right dosage of liquid courage in my system. I think I even made Lolo blush at that point.

'Ja jo, o montle,' he said softly biting his bottom lip.

We looked up at the sky, listening to the background sounds of the heavy base that had hypnotised a room full of thirsty youths. He lit the remainder of the joint we were smoking earlier on, and I coughed a little less this time. I rested my head on his shoulder, slipping deeper into my own thoughts. Lolo was right – being out with him was fun.

'Lolo,' I said, lifting my head.

He turned to me and his small reddened eyes met mine.

'Do you love me?' I whispered.

Lolo paused for a second, making what could have been a beautiful moment very uncomfortable. I saw a smile beginning to peek out of the corners of his lips. A gentle laugh escaped his throat, and he took a final drag of the joint. Streams of smoke passed through his lips and disappeared into the air.

'Yoh jo, you're high,' he said, continuing to laugh.

Yes, he was right. I could feel it now. I was high.

Moleta ngwedi, o leta lefifi

*The one who waits for the moon,
too waits for darkness*

I found Dineo outside, her forehead glistening with sweat. Her light-skinned face had turned reddish, while her sinuses had yet to adjust to the dust invasion she had to suffer through almost daily, all in the name of sweeping. She hobbled her exhausted body into the bathroom, and locked herself inside. When I walked back into the house after polishing the stoep, Mama was enjoying her tea, reading her Bible at the kitchen table.

'Go and take twenty rand from my purse o lo reka magwinya,' Mama ordered while pouring a bit of her tea into the saucer from her 'Jesus ♥s You' mug.

I nodded but remained seated. Mama looked at me strangely.

'Aren't you going to buy magwinya?' she asked.

'I think Dineo is bathing. I'm just waiting for her to finish,' I said.

'Go, it's not far. You'll bath when you come back.'

I shifted slowly out of my chair. Mama never allowed me out of the house before I'd bathed.

I walked with the broadest smile, greeting every familiar and unfamiliar face I came across. The smell of snoek and vetkoek danced on my senses.

When I was about three streets away from Ndende Street on my way back, there they were. Sis' Nozipho and Lolo were standing so close they could probably taste each other's breath.

Lolo was slowly retreating from Sis' Nozipho's arms when he spotted me. He froze. I froze. A timer went on in both of our minds counting us down . . .

On your marks . . .

Get set . . .

Ready . . .

Fire . . .

Go!

I immediately took off sprinting, with Lolo chasing after me.

'Naledi, Naledi, maan!' Lolo shouted, running behind me.

Lolo was about as fast as any twenty-three-year-old athletic soccer boy could be, so I really didn't get very far. He caught me, grabbing hold of my arm just before I could get to our gate.

'Ke u bone, Lolo!'

'Shh, so why are you screaming for everyone to hear you?'

'What do you think you're doing?'

'That's none of your business!'

'Oho! It's all a game to you, isn't it? Everything is one big fat joke!'

'Naledi, why are you taking this so personal?'

I paused and collected myself.

'You're going to get beaten, Lolo. Why would you even be

busy with her here, where people can see you? What if Bra Joe caught you?'

'What did you even see, huh? You saw nothing. Stop acting like the people of Ndende Street, always jumping to conclusions when you see two people standing and talking.'

'Lolo, this is not just some girl or one of your groupies. She's married and much, much, much older than you. Have a little respect for yourself,' I said.

'Wena, you are preaching to me about self-respect? Go and look at yourself first in the mirror before you give me the holier-than-thou speech. You can fool them all, but you forget that I know you!'

I raised my finger and pointed it in Lolo's face. I was about to cuss him out when I heard, 'Naledi le Lolo, what are you doing?'

It was Mama.

Mama didn't even allow me to take two steps into the house before yelling: 'Keo o busy le basimane ko diterateng. She is wearing yesterday's panty, she hasn't even bathed but she is standing in the streets talking to boys. Sies! How many times must I tell you about that boy?'

'Bathong, Mama, it's just Lolo. These two grew up together,' Dineo defended me.

'It's because you haven't been around. You haven't heard ditaba tsa Lolo. You haven't seen the things that he does,' Mama continued.

Eventually, it was magwinya and snoek that calmed Mama down.

Mama went to bed early that night. Dineo suddenly reduced the volume on the TV in the middle of the biggest scene in the movie. I knew what was going to happen next because I had watched *The Color Purple* a million times, but I didn't care. I still needed to watch Celie put a knife under Albert's throat. I wanted to say it too with that southern accent that I was now starting to master – 'Until you do right by me, everything you even think about gonna fail' – and then silently applaud the power of Whoopi Goldberg's performance on the inside.

I was on my feet, irritated. I wasn't in the mood for another weird attempt by my mother at bonding. I moved across towards Dineo to snatch the remote from her hand when she asked, 'Naledi, wena le Lolo la jola?'

I stopped, then began to retreat slowly back to where I had been sitting.

'Naledi, is Lolo—'

'For the hundredth time, no!' I said before Dineo could finish her sentence.

Dineo exhaled a deep sigh of relief. I had missed my favourite scene.

*   *   *

After class, Minnie and I walked down the art department's corridor, admiring the latest colourful murals, until we reached the classroom at the very end of the passage. Itu and her artwork made a beautiful contrast with the room where everything was painted white, including the floors. Itu wore a big

African-print turban with a white overall that was covered in splashes of paint.

I turned down the volume on the CD player before sitting on one of the tables that were pushed up against the wall. Dineo's question about Lolo was still bothering me.

'Why are love and sex and even topics that matter to girls so difficult for black people to talk about?' Itu and Minnie seemed a little thrown by my question, so I tried to phrase it differently. 'Why do we struggle so much to have open and honest conversations about anything connected to the opposite sex with people who are older than us in black households?'

'Well, we do have conversations. It's just that black people wait until bridal showers and even until the actual wedding day. Then only do they put non-virgins in a room and give them advice on how to please their men and what it means to be a woman.' Itu's voice carried over Simphiwe Dana's; she always played Simphiwe Dana's music while she worked. She said she wanted to be one with the songstress so that Dana's music could infect her artwork with her genius.

'Let's also not forget that these talks do still take place in initiation schools. The thing is, we've become so western that we are destroying the very structures that were put in place to answer such questions. And more especially for us girls – there are different rites of passage that we just don't do any more, not understanding that there are valuable teachings we are losing along the way, all in the name of following a culture-less white man's religion.'

'Excuse me, but the church *does* teach about sex, we just

218

choose not to listen,' Minnie added, once again trying to maintain the integrity of her beliefs against Itu.

'Standing in a pulpit and telling me that fornication is a sin and then quoting a scripture is not preparing me, nor is it teaching me anything about the realities of becoming a woman. It doesn't magically shut down everything I experience or feel. It doesn't stop me from being curious. It doesn't stop me from being horny. It doesn't stop my breasts from growing. It doesn't stop guys from finding me desirable. It certainly doesn't stop women from being violated. The only thing that it has done successfully is to silence us. And we are all sitting in church and at our dinner tables pretending to be okay when we are really not!' I said, purging from the place of confusion and conflict where I had often found myself.

I glanced at Itu's painting. The image had taken on the form of an afro-headed black girl, standing in the middle of a squatter camp. When I looked closely, I could see she was disfigured on one side of her strikingly beautiful face.

I could see myself on that canvas. I was a girl from the ghetto, whose beauty and wounds had been crafted by her environment. And I knew that was the story of all three of us sitting in that room.

Lijingi lidliwa yinhlitiyo

Sour porridge is eaten by the heart

When Professor Addington made the announcement, it was like a bomb exploding in my lap.

'Rehearsals will no longer end at five but at nine-thirty,' he'd said.

I was halfway out of the door in the morning when I informed Dineo of this.

'Naledi, come back here!' Dineo shouted.

I wished she would lower her voice. The last thing I needed was Mama rushing into the kitchen to see what was happening. Dineo did find a workable solution before Mama caught sight of our discussion, though. She would speak to Kedi on my behalf, and Kedi and Sol would pick me up from school that night.

When they arrived at nine-thirty, Sol, surprisingly, was not playing his window-rattling base music. The music mellowed the tension simmering in his and Kedi's conversation. 'Sokwenzenjani' featuring Robbie Malinga filled the car as I got in.

'Solomon, re nyala neng mara? My mother is asking when

we are getting married and I can't blame her because ho neng re jola – it's been years now.'

When Kedi called Sol by his full name, 'Solomon', I knew that she meant business, even through her calm tone of voice.

'So now we must rush? We must choke ourselves in debt because your mother wants a wedding, haai maan ema hanyane, Kedi.'

'Bathong, Solomon, at least ntsa mahadi, even if it's just half. Give something – even a letter to my parents to show that you are serious about me.'

I sat quietly in the backseat, using my fingers to try to count the number of years that Sol and Kedi had been dating. It could have been seven or eight years already.

'Nna shame askies, I'm sorry, but you won't rush me. That you won't do!'

'Eleven years kaofela, Solomon, and you're still talking about being rushed?'

It was much, much longer than I had thought.

'You and your family will not pressure me,' Sol said stubbornly.

'Mxm, fok maan, Solomon,' Kedi said quietly, throwing her hand in the air and turning to look out of the window.

'Le wena fok,' Sol responded, also in a calm tone.

It could have been the fact that I was present that this argument turned out to be more of what Itu and her SRC people would describe as a 'robust discussion' rather than a fight. By the time they dropped me off at home, the pair was laughing and still singing along to Robbie Malinga's music.

'Eh, Naledi, mara wa di jaja tse? You kids of today know nothing about good music,' Sol said to me, showing off what he viewed as his brilliant musical taste. I simply smiled and let him have his moment.

When I arrived home at ten o'clock, Mama was still up.

'What time does school end?' she asked, staring at me like she wanted to slap me into a coma.

Recognising the look on Mama's face, Dineo quickly said, 'She's got rehearsals for that play they are doing, so sometimes she's going to come home late.'

'Don't tell me about plays. Is it decent for a schoolgirl to be coming home at this hour?'

I knew at that moment that this would not unfold like Kedi and Sol's 'robust discussion', but this was rather going to turn out as one hostile showdown.

'And then when does she do her homework? When does she cook, and who must get on their knees and polish that stoep for her?' said Mama, her voice rising.

'Mama, leave Naledi alone. If she feels she can handle it, then let her. Give her space to do so.'

'Kana, Naledi is not my child,' Mama said, throwing her hands in the air. 'So what say do I have in her well-being? It's not like I'm the one who raised her while you were off running wild with that hyena that killed your child!'

Mama hit a blow that even made me shudder. Dineo said nothing. Instead, she walked away.

Mama lowered her voice and addressed me firmly: 'Hear me when I say this: a girl does not do as she pleases, Naledi.

You do not walk into the house whenever it suits you. One day you will be married. Are these the things that you are going to do in your marriage? This will not happen, not in my house!'

Umuthi ugotshwe usemanzi

The branch is bent while it's still young

We were running the 'Meadowlands' routine. I touched my forehead to pretend that a fever was coming on, and missed a step or two to give the effect that my body was not fully engaging. When everyone would drop to the ground, I would be a beat behind them, and by the time the five o'clock break came, Professor Addington had picked up that I was not feeling well.

'Okay, let's break and at six we start with the second half of the show. Naledi, can I see you quickly.'

The other students scattered out of the rehearsal room.

'You seem off today,' said Professor Addington. 'Is everything okay?'

Professor Addington was very flamboyant for a man in his late sixties. Standing before him I wondered if Mama would ban me from participating in the musical if she knew that Prof Addington was a sinner of the highest form. Would she chastise me for holding a chain-smoking gay man in such high regard? Everything in me wanted to be there. The stage was the only place where I actually felt like I belonged. But I had

224

a curfew. And besides curfew, I had responsibilities. If I explained this to him, he'd just replace me.

'Everything is fine, Prof. I just felt dizzy, but I'm fine now,' I said to him.

I had worked way too hard to ruin my chances because I was someone's future wife in training.

'Naledi, are you sure?' he asked again.

'Actually, Prof, I don't know how I'm going to get home tonight. I want to stay till the end, especially because we don't have much time left before we open, but I'm worried that there won't be any taxis at that hour.'

'I'm sure there's someone around who lives in Soweto who can offer you a ride home for tonight. Don't worry – I'll organise it for you.'

Did that man know that there were more people living in Soweto than the entire population of people in some small countries? Did he know that it was quicker to get to town than to go from one end of Soweto to the other? Did he know that there were various routes of getting in and out of Soweto depending on where you lived?

'Okay . . .' I nodded.

'Come now, Ledi, let's go get you something to eat for that dizziness.'

We walked to the cafeteria, where Professor Addington bought me a sandwich and bottled water. When we rehearsed the second half of the show, I was on form. I was so focused that by the end of it my back was sweating, my muscles were aching and my forehead was dripping.

We had an orchestra for the production. Sometimes they rehearsed with us in the theatre. Other times, like today, they held separate rehearsals in the music department. It was very easy to ignore Sizwe in a room that had such a big cast.

Mthi, one of the music lecturers and the musical director of the show, was a thirty-something-year-old black man who apparently lived in Soweto. He had offered to take me home but was sure to inform Professor Addington to notify me that his rehearsal would be ending at ten.

I walked into the music room, where students were sitting behind their music stands, sheet music in front of them, and instruments in their hands. I sat in the front of the class trying to avoid looking in Sizwe's direction. It was quite embarrassing to be propped up there like a child who had been punished for misbehaving in class. I failed to focus on the beauty of the music being played, distracted by Sizwe, who would often glance at me. He looked just as beautiful blowing into the trumpet as he did playing the saxophone. He made everything look effortless.

'Sorry, Mthi, but something sounded completely off.' Sizwe jumped up and halted the song.

Everyone in the room listened to Sizwe without objection, including Mthi.

'Alright, um, yeah, Sizwe, I heard that too,' said Mthi. 'Let's take that from the top, guys. Strings – I feel like I'm losing you in some parts.'

Sizwe's discipline when it came to his craft and his confidence were the sexiest things about him besides his good looks.

I understood why Itu found him to be arrogant. I thought back to when I got to know him during our quiet afternoons spent with him playing his instrument and me digging into my monologue. It was his talent that had drawn me towards him, but at the time, I had thought it was *my talent* that had pulled him towards me. After what had happened between us, I wasn't so sure any more. I wasn't sure of who Sizwe was. Was he the passionate musician who bled music or the play-boy who had hit it and run?

Forty minutes later, I was still sitting in the music room, when Professor Addington walked in with a panicked Dineo. I quickly gathered my things and rushed out. I could tell by how fast Dineo was walking towards Sol's car that she was furious. Dineo hopped into the passenger seat and I jumped into the back. Kedi was a much more careful driver than her boyfriend, who sped through the streets like a delinquent at times. That could also be because Kedi had just recently got her driver's licence so she drove as slowly and as care-fully as Moruti. It didn't take Dineo long before she started yelling at me.

'Naledi, wa gafa na? Mama's blood pressure is sky-high! How were you going to come back home? You have a phone but you don't even have the decency to call and let us know that you are okay or that you are stuck at school. What use is a phone if you don't use it?'

Once Dineo gave me a chance to speak, I explained that I couldn't just bail on rehearsals. She said that I could no longer rehearse till late, as per the agreement with my grandmother.

I told her that I'd never agreed to that. She thought I was being rude. I then explained that we had only two weeks left before opening night – skipping rehearsals was not an option. And that's when she hit me with the question: 'And then – Mama?'

'Tell her, Dineo. Tell her that I need to rehearse otherwise I'll get kicked out of the show!'

'Eish, eish, Naledi,' Dineo said, shaking her head in frustration. 'You want to start a war between us? You forget that that is not my house. We are basically living off her pensioner's grant at the moment. What do you want me to do, Naledi, huh, what?'

Silence.

I didn't have a response for my mother. I understood her position, but I needed her to understand mine.

'It's just for this week and next week only, Dineo, please,' I said.

'Why don't the two of you stay with me until the show is over?' said Kedi. 'You'll explain to your mother that you are looking for a job, and we've got a car which makes things easier for you.'

When we got home, Mama was standing at the front door, waiting to breathe fire in my direction.

'Naledi, what has got into you?' she barked the minute we opened the door. 'You shave off your hair and suddenly you think that makes you a man. You think you can do as you please in this house? If that's what you think, then get your things and get out of your grandfather's house and go build yourself a shack somewhere else!'

'She tried but couldn't leave rehearsals – her lecturer wouldn't allow it,' said Dineo.

Mama seemed to buy the story and headed towards the sink to get herself some water to calm herself down. Dineo sat at the kitchen table, then cleared her throat.

'Um, Mama, I think it will be best if Naledi and I stayed with Kedibone until this show of hers is done. It will make things easy,' she said.

Mama threw the glass into the sink. 'Kedibone? Naledi is going nowhere, especially not near that girl!'

'It will also be good for me while I look for a job, you know,' Dineo continued.

I was still standing a few centimetres from the door, just in case my grandmother came after me.

'Doesn't Kedibone live with a boyfriend now?' said Mama.

'They plan on getting married soon, Mama.'

'Vat en sit, ke vat en sit – don't try and colour it!' Mama shouted. 'You want to take this child and teach her sin by throwing her into the devil's schemes. If Naledi's teacher doesn't understand that a girl cannot be out in the streets and walking into the house at ten at night, then Naledi must study something else. Clearly, this *thing* is coming with bad habits.'

The more my grandmother spoke, the more I felt like I was a bubbling pot. I wanted her to be quiet. I wanted her to consider me and how I was feeling for once in my life. What about the things that I wanted?

Mama turned back to me and said, 'You are done with this play thing. Go and tell your teacher that!'

She walked into her bedroom and just like that the discussion was over. She had to have the final word.

I couldn't stop my tears from escaping.

'Askies, Naledi, askies,' said Dineo. 'Don't cry. There will be other plays and other opportunities to act and do these things, o ska lla tlhe.'

That's all it was to Dineo and Mama – just a play. Just one of those things I did to pass the time until something more serious came along. Mama didn't even care how this would affect my marks. She couldn't stop to consider how many years I had been working towards this moment.

I opened the kitchen door and ran out to lock myself in the outdoor toilet.

Dineo followed, and I could hear her hit her hand against the door. 'Naledi, Naledi, open. Naledi, please open. Let's talk,' she pleaded.

I could hear Mama's voice shouting: 'What is wrong with that child? Why is she bringing us such acts at this time of the night?'

I knew that I couldn't stay in there the entire night. I knew that at some point I would have to come out and face my grandmother. But I stayed in the toilet until I had no more tears left. Mama stopped shouting from her bedroom. Dineo was sitting in the cold, alone in the dark on the stoep. Her eyes were glistening.

'I'm sorry, Naledi,' she said again.

I sat down next to her, feeling the weight of my reddened eyes. Dineo stretched out her arm and placed it around my shoulders. She moved her body closer towards me. This felt odd. I got up just as quickly as she had attempted to embrace me.

I slept on the living room floor next to Dineo with a wide distance separating our bodies. Those hours spent apart from Mama didn't lessen the tension in the kitchen the next morning. My grandmother broke the silence when we were almost finished eating our porridge.

'Watseba, Naledi, you scare me,' Mama said.

Dineo remained just as quiet as I was. Mama took one last spoon of porridge, then got up from her seat. Instead of taking her bowl to the sink, she came towards me. She leaned over, with her body towering above me.

'You've changed. You even look different. You are not the same child that I raised.'

My throat went dry.

Nawa ri la rivhanzhi, u zwimbela dzi a talula

We can all eat beans but when it comes to bloating, they choose who suffers

From inside the theatre I could see the sky was now completely dark. I had received a call from Dineo earlier that day telling me that she wouldn't be coming back home. I should have told her right then that I wouldn't make it back any time before Mama's bedtime, never mind before sunset. I kept my eyes peeled on the clock. I couldn't hear a word that Professor Addington was saying. It was nine-thirty and I was still sitting in a theatre in the north of Johannesburg – nowhere near home.

'Ledi, are you okay?'

'Huh?'

'Prof said call time is four o'clock tomorrow,' one of my cast mates said.

I bolted backstage to change out of my costume and to grab my bag.

As if things couldn't get any worse, on my way out of the dressing room, Sizwe was there, standing in front of me.

He moved closer towards me. I took three steps back. He

stopped. Then I stopped. He moved in again, only this time he was able to reach me before I could get away. He pulled me in and embraced me. His scent was exactly the same – a smell of masculinity roped into a beautiful fragrance. I wanted to fight and push him away, but instead I found myself clutching on to him as tightly as he was holding me. He cupped my cheeks and drew me in for a kiss on the lips. Soft and delicate. 'Naledi,' he said, 'I'm proud of you. I watched you rehearse tonight and the way you sing and dance and deliver each line, you're incredible.'

Sizwe had called me by my full name, Naledi, and it had never felt so right. In that moment, he had validated my dream. Without my having to say it, Sizwe walked away, knowing that I had forgiven him for being so thoughtless with my heart.

I dashed out of the theatre with my bag slung on my back, running through the streets, not stopping to wait for cars before crossing the road. Some motorists hooted, some cursed at me, but I needed to make that last taxi. I didn't stop to see who or what was standing in the dark corners and creeping in the alleyways.

The last taxi to Pimville only had four passengers including myself. The driver wanted to wait for a few minutes in the hope of getting more customers, but for the first time in my life I become vocal in a taxi.

'Please, I pray, I need to get home,' I said to the driver.

He looked at me. I knew exactly where his mind was going

233

when he said, 'Fine, I'll leave on condition that you come sit in the front.'

My first rule on 'How to handle a taxi experience 101' was that I never, under any circumstances, sat in the front seat. This was only because there was nothing worse than having to count the change. But seeing that there were only four of us, surely I could easily do the math, right?

I opened the front door and hoisted myself onto the high seat. Once I was finished handing the driver the exact amount of money he expected from four people, he turned down the radio. As he drove, he would look at the road, glance at me, then back to the road.

'What's your name?' he finally asked through a very thick isiZulu accent.

'Palesa,' I said without turning my head to face him.

Second rule: always lie about your name and everything else about you to strange people in the taxi.

'Palesa, Palesa . . . from where?'

I looked out of the window, pretending like I hadn't heard him. He asked again, placing his hand on my thigh this time. I wanted to jump out but it was after ten o'clock at night. I wished the other passengers would say something, but their silence was very telling of how they were worried that, if they spoke up, they would most likely find themselves stranded on the freeway.

'I live around Zone 2,' I told him.

He changed gear and placed his hand back on my thigh, squeezing it.

'Umuhle yazi?' There was that loaded question again. 'You're very beautiful, you know that?' Those same words that Vuyani had said to me before I woke up naked in his bed.

'Kea leboga,' I responded in Setswana, hoping that that would turn him off me. It was often said that taxi drivers wanted people to speak isiZulu to them and not other languages because they were tribalists who believed in the superiority of their language and culture. But no, speaking Setswana had the opposite effect on that man.

He clapped his hands, rubbed them against each other, and remarked, 'Ow madoda! Oh, here's a flower from the Batswana people whose tongue has made my heart skip a beat.'

'Sho't left,' one of the passengers shouted.

Two people jumped off, leaving just one more person and me. I was still a distance away from home.

'How old are you?' he asked.

I had to keep my composure. I had to do everything I could not to upset him.

Third rule: do not piss off the driver!

Another stereotype about taxi drivers was that they were all temperamental, inconsiderate, reckless hooligans who carried guns.

'I'm sixteen,' I said.

He scoffed. 'With such big breasts and fresh thighs *and* you are travelling at night by yourself, I'm sure you are twenty-five.'

I hadn't removed my makeup after the dress rehearsal, so that wasn't doing me any favours.

'No, seriously, I'm sixteen.'

He laughed again. 'Su' dlala ngami, I can see that you are lying. What, you don't want me to visit you?'

'Passage,' the last passenger shouted.

I began to weigh my options: do I get off with the last passenger and walk twice the distance to get home in the dark (which was still dangerous), or do I stay alone in a taxi with a man who had thirst seeping through his eyes?

The taxi slowed down and eventually came to a stop. The guy sitting at the back slid open the door, and without another thought, I opened my door, jumped out and walked.

'Ulale kahle, baby, or how do the Tswanas say it? O robale sentle, dream about me tonight.' He poked his head through the rolled-down window and continued to watch me. 'Ow madoda, I haven't seen a bum that big and thighs that ripe all day. We thank the Tswana god for creating such a beautiful woman, ow siyabonga Khama!'

As soon as I heard the sound of the taxi taking off, I kicked rocks and raised dust with my sprinting feet, running as fast as my legs could carry me. All I could hear was the sound of distant cars, my breath, and my feet on the ground. It was at times such as these that I remembered the scriptures my grandmother had taught me. Only God would get me home unscathed.

'Who shall separate us from the love of Christ? Shall tribulation, or distress, or persecution, or famine, or nakedness, or peril, or sword? As it is written, For thy sake we are being killed all the day long; we are accounted as sheep for the slaughter. Nay, in all these things we are more than conquerors through Him who loved us. For I am sure that neither death nor life, nor angels nor rulers, nor things present, nor things to come, nor powers, nor height, nor depth, nor anything else in all creation, will be able to separate us from the love of God.'

I had lost count of how many times I had recited the scripture before entering Ndende Street. I was breathless. My chest was burning. Our street had never looked so splendid with all its potholes.

I stuck my hand in to open the gate, but the gate was locked. The lights in and around the house were switched off. I reached for my cellphone in my backpack and saw the eight missed calls from my grandmother and the final message that read: *Don't come back. Sleep in the streets where you are. Ong' tl-wayela gampe!*

With the street dark and deserted, my distress returned.

I called Lolo three times before he eventually answered his phone, sounding groggy. Since when did Lolo sleep before midnight?

After doing a lot of convincing, Lolo appeared dressed in a navy gown, white socks and slippers.

'Naledi, keng jo, so late?' he asked, not trying to hide the irritation in his voice.

'Lolo, Mama locked me out and she's not letting me in.'

'And what do you expect me to do?'

'Can I sleep in your room, please?'

'Yoh, Naledi!' he said, interlocking his fingers behind his head. 'And then what happens tomorrow?'

'Please, Lolo, I'll deal with tomorrow when it comes.'

Lolo was silent for a moment, then said, 'Throw me your bag over the fence and I'll show you where you can jump over.'

I tossed my bag over to him. He directed me to the corner of the wall and guided me through the process like someone who had done this quite a number of times himself. Lolo caught me on the other side and helped me down. Tiptoeing, we made our way to his room.

Lolo took off his gown and slippers. He stood topless, his dark chocolate frame muscled. Soccer was doing amazing things for him – and his body.

Lolo got into bed while I stripped down almost completely naked, leaving only my underwear on. I put on the T-shirt that he had lent me before slipping under the covers. Lolo's eyes were already shut, but I couldn't fall asleep. Many things were going through my mind, including the play and Mama. Dineo had defended me on many occasions lately, but I wasn't sure if she would have my back on this one. I hadn't been the nicest person to her either.

I was also thinking about the person whose bed I was sharing.

'Lolo. Lolo . . .' I tapped him on the shoulder. 'Lolo. Lolo.'

No response.

I tapped him again. 'Lolo.'

'Naledi, I want to sleep!'

I was a little startled by Lolo's outburst, but we had some

issues we needed to address and I couldn't just pretend like everything was fine between us.

'Lolo, how do you sleep with your own mother?'

Lolo raised his upper body, turning it towards me. Even though the room was dark, I could see the scowl on his face.

'You and Sis' Nozipho – how could you sleep with her? That's disgusting,' I said. I wasn't going to let Lolo's reaction intimidate me into keeping quiet.

'So Nozipho is my mother? Entlek uzama ho reng?'

'See, that's the problem, when you go from calling someone older than you "Sis' Nozipho" to just "Nozipho". We call our fathers just by their names, they are no longer abuti or ntate. That's how the lines get blurred – next thing we're sleeping with them.'

'And then wena, what do *you* call your own mother? You're a hypocrite, jo! You must take a very good look at me, Naledi. I'm not Minnie or Dineo who has sex with anything that moves!'

My hand landed hard on Lolo's face. I felt the sting on my palm. Lolo recoiled, with his hand holding his cheek. I got up, and switched on the light. Lolo sprang out of the bed towards me to switch the light back off.

'Wahlanya, Naledi?'

'How dare you insult my mother!'

Lolo and I went back and forth in a whispered fight before he relented.

'Okay, askies, I shouldn't have mentioned your mother, and you're right, I shouldn't have been messing around with Nozipho. But she came after me and I'm a guy – what am I supposed to do? I mean, Bra Joe has kids all over the place; she also needed to have her fun.'

'Sis' Nozipho is a mother. She must have a little bit more respect for herself and her kids. How do you think her kids are feeling with people going around saying their mother is busy sleeping around with a child?'

'I'm not a child, Naledi,' Lolo quickly retorted.

'Well, then stop acting like one!'

I was tired of fighting with Lolo and I got the sense that he felt the same.

'Please, let's sleep,' he whispered, stretching out his hand. I placed my hand in his and allowed him to lead us back to bed.

* * *

'Lehlohonolo, Lehlohonolo!'

It was the way in which Lolo kicked off the duvet cover that brought a sudden end to my dream. I wasn't much of a runner; it felt as though my legs were in shock from running all those kilometres. Exhausted, my body had failed to wake up on time.

'Lehlohonolo!'

I jumped out of the bed. Lolo and I paced about the room frantically. I was looking for my leggings, my T-shirt, my All Stars, my socks and my backpack. Lolo was trying to find his phone, his flip-flops, and a clear mind, which neither of us had.

'Lehlohonolo, do you not having training to get to? Did

you see what time it is?' MaKarabo continued to hammer on the door with her hand.

'Ja, Ma, I overslept but I'm up,' said Lolo.

Lolo and I kept our voices low all the while trying to dress without making a noise, but it was almost impossible to get it together without raising any eyebrows.

'Lehlohonolo, who are you talking to?'

Lolo and I froze.

'Hey wena, Lehlohonolo, do you have someone in there? Open this damn door before I break it down!'

MaKarabo was not one to get angry and I finally understood why. Anger did not sound good on her.

We could hear Ntate Moloi's voice approaching the door. 'MaKarabo, keng?' he asked.

'Get me the spare keys from the house,' MaKarabo ordered.

But Ntate Moloi must have refused, because I heard MaKarabo say, 'Fine then I'll get them myself!'

Lolo placed his hands on his head and started pacing around. I needed him to act before his mother opened the door to find the two of us half-naked.

'Lolo, do something!' I shouted, forgetting that raising my voice was probably not the best idea.

'Be quiet le wena, Naledi, I'm trying to think!'

Just then, I heard the keys turning and the door swing open. MaKarabo clutched a belt in her hand.

'Na-le-di!' she said, aghast.

Ntate Moloi was much calmer than MaKarabo but just as appalled. 'Manyala,' he said, shaking his head in disbelief.

Lolo stepped in front of his mother, ready to explain, but before he could let out two words to speak, MaKarabo flung that belt in her hand across Lolo's naked torso. The force was so strong that I could hear the belt moving through the air before landing on Lolo. Lolo crouched on contact. MaKarabo pushed Lolo to the side and charged towards me. I leapt onto the bed to flee the raging woman, but she kept on swinging and I kept on ducking. I felt a swipe across my back. It set fire to my skin. Lolo ran out of the room; I followed behind him. Ntate Moloi just stood back and watched from afar.

'How dare you bring such filth into my house! You think this is a brothel that you can have sex with each other in the blankets that I bought and that I wash with my own hands!' MaKarabo yelled as she chased us through every corner of her yard.

My limbs had very little speed left in them. I just couldn't run any more. I leaned against the fence, fighting to catch my breath. I looked up and saw the many faces that had gathered in the street to watch the spectacle unfold.

Across our wire fence, there she was, standing with her eyes fixed on me. Mama remained expressionless, staring at me wearing only a T-shirt that barely covered my thighs. It was exposing my panties for every perverted eye and gossiping tongue to burp up later at their dinner tables.

MaKarabo threw her belt onto the ground and stormed off into the house with Ntate Moloi walking behind her. Mama, too, turned and walked back inside.

* * *

Lolo came rushing towards me. He took me by the hand and pulled me back to his room.

I sobbed, curled up on Lolo's bed like a wounded little girl, locked in his embrace, until Ntate Moloi walked in. We both broke free of each other and sat upright. Ntate Moloi pulled out a chair, and sat facing us. We were both quiet, waiting for him to say something.

Finally, Ntate Moloi spoke.

'Naledi, I've known Mme Norah for many years. I know how she raised you. Myself and MaKarabo have been parents to you. Why would the two of you behave like this?' he asked.

Lolo tried to interject. 'But, Ntate—'

'Wait, Lehlohonolo, wait, I'm still talking,' he said. 'I've been watching the two of you lately. You have become a law unto yourselves. I'm not interested in the details. I don't want to know them, so please respect me as your father and spare me.'

But Lolo still felt that the facts were important. That the punishment we had been dealt did not fit the crime.

'Mara Ntate, MaKarabo believes that we were busy here last night and that's not true,' Lolo explained.

'It doesn't matter, Lehlohonolo!' Ntate Moloi said sternly. 'Naledi was not supposed to have been here in the first place! So when everyone is sleeping, you two are jumping walls and running around, and we must be calm and say it's fine because you didn't sleep with each other?'

Lolo kept his head down.

Ntate Moloi wanted an answer. 'Is it fine for you to have a

243

girl who is not your wife sleeping in your father's house? Are you a married man na, Lehlohonolo?'

'Che Ntate, I'm not,' Lolo responded.

Ntate Moloi got up, leaving us with a veil of guilt hanging over us.

* * *

Lolo went to get me a big silver metal tub and boiling water in an urn. He sat down on the bed while I took a bath.

As I poured the water onto my bruises, I could feel every sting and burn. I groaned. Lolo moved down, took the wash-cloth from my hands and began to dab gently on my wounds.

There was something about sitting in a tub completely na-ked with Lolo trying to clean my cuts that unlocked my tears again. I wasn't crying about MaKarabo or Mama. I had been battered and disgraced long before that morning. I had been running scared with no end in sight, way before I had found myself running terrified alone in the dark through the streets the previous night.

'Someone raped me . . .' I whispered.

Lolo stopped cleaning me. He rested his back against the wall, and I shared with him the pain that I had carried since the day I had woken up in Vuyani's bed.

Eventually, he stood up and left. I got out of the tub. I got dressed, then sat alone in his room for more than two hours, staring blankly at the wall.

Lolo walked in with a plastic bag in his hand. I could smell it before he opened the bag. Magwinya le snoek fish.

'I thought you'd be hungry,' he said, passing one to me.

I laughed softly. When we were finished eating, Lolo placed his arm around me and pulled me towards him, my head pressed against his chest.

'I'm so sorry, Naledi . . .'

I tilted my head, looking up at him. His eyes were beginning to tear up.

That day was the first time I had seen Lolo cry. Not even at his own sister's funeral had his tears escaped him.

I sat between his legs, facing him, brushing each tear gently away with my fingertips. I could no longer deny it.

'Lehlohonolo, I'm in love with you.'

As unsure as I was about what his reaction would be and how this declaration would affect our friendship moving forwards, I had to tell him.

Lolo smiled. A very naughty smile.

'Wang' shela jo, nine-nine?'

'Yes jo, I'm asking you to be my boyfriend, nine-nine.'

Lolo leaned in and kissed me. I knew without question that I was loved in the same way, if not more.

* * *

Clement was outside chilling with Thiza on the old car seat cooling themselves down from the scorching November heat with a ngud' and Courtleigh each in their hands. Thiza made it no secret that he and Clement were talking about us as Lolo and I walked out of the Moloi household, hand in hand after that morning's showdown.

'Uh, Lolo mfethu onesibindi ngempela! That's the only untouched girl here on our street because everyone is terrified of Mme Norah. Uh, well done, boy, sho nja yam',' Thiza said, congratulating Lolo on having managed to get me into bed.

'Nxa, drunken fool,' I hissed underneath my breath.

Lolo gripped my hand tighter and walked more hurriedly, wanting to get me away and into a taxi as soon as possible. My decision to go to campus rather than to go home was just a tactic to buy me more time.

Sizwe was waiting to greet me before the start of rehearsal. He was working overtime to get back into my good graces. I used this to get him to talk to Mthi for me. It turned out Mthi lived in Diepkloof, just a stone's throw away from Pimville, and said he would bring me home every day until the run of our show was over.

Sizwe walked me to Mthi's car, carrying my bag after rehearsal. 'Please make sure that she gets home safe,' he said to Mthi while opening the passenger door for me. I should have told him that he really didn't have to trouble himself; I was so smitten over my new boyfriend that everything that had happened between us was now water under the bridge. But there was a part of me that thoroughly enjoyed seeing Sizwe panting after me like a dog in need of water.

Mthi insisted on accompanying me into the house. He thought it would be decent to introduce himself, considering his new responsibility of ensuring my safe arrival home. It was almost ten-thirty at night. Mama was already in bed, thankfully, and like butter on hot bread, Dineo melted under Mthi's charm. To be fair on Dineo, Mthi had also suddenly developed some sort of stutter when he spoke to my mother. 'Hi, um . . . I'm . . . I'm Naledi's lecturer, not really her lecturer because I happen to teach music but, yes, I'm the musical director for the show, so yeah. Oh yes, I'm . . . I'm Zola Mthi.'

'Hi Zola.' Dineo pulled out her dazzling white smile while shaking his hand.

Even on a shabby day wearing a pair of pantyhose on her head and a gown, Dineo still had the same effect on men.

Mthi was hardly out of the gate and I had yet to put my bag down when Dineo threw out of the dreaded question at me.

'Naledi, o robala le Lolo?'

I didn't respond.

'Naledi, nkarabe, o robala le Lolo na?' she asked again.

I couldn't run this time. My only alternative was to go to the bedroom where Mama was, and that was out of the question.

'Yes,' I said.

Dineo went quiet. She got up and started preparing the place where we would sleep by laying out the mattress and blankets on the floor as if I had not just dropped a bomb. Lying next to her not knowing what she was thinking about my admission of sleeping with the boy next door was probably the worst kind of punishment.

In the morning, things were no better with Mama sitting at the table with us. Mama wouldn't look at me. We ate our porridge in silence, and when I was finished eating, I took my bag and left for school, only to return home long after dark.

Pula! Ha ene

Let it rain

Mama and I had moved around each other like two strangers without the greetings people normally passed on in the mornings. We got dressed in the same room. We ate our porridge, had our dinners and drank our tea at the same table. But nothing was said.

Mama reached to open the door to leave and I quickly ran up behind her with my Bible in my hand.

'Where are you going?' Those were the first words that Mama had spoken to me in almost five days. What came out of her mouth next made me wish she had stayed silent. 'You hate God and you have proven that. So what makes you think that I would walk into church with Satan by my side?'

Mama walked out and slammed the door behind her. I stood for nearly twenty minutes staring at the closed kitchen door, holding my Bible.

I wasn't surprised to find Lolo home alone. He and Dineo had a few things in common, including the fact that they wouldn't be able to describe what the inside of a church looked like, they had not set foot in one in so long. Lolo rubbed his hand on the top of my head after placing his soft lips against mine. He had a romantic idea of us sitting side by side under the gazebo just down the street, getting our hair cut together.

'There's nothing romantic about that, Lolo.'

'I thought girls like it when their man gives them money to do their hair. It's fifty rand for chiskop, hundred and fifty if you want a fancy brush cut. Or what, would you prefer to go get your hair cut by Nozipho?'

There was no way I was going to set foot in Sis' Nozipho's salon. I also needed to distract myself from the drama with my grandmother, and since Lolo was paying, I couldn't say no.

Having my hair cut, out in the open on the street corner like that, was a completely different experience. Very different from the hen house to which I had become accustomed. There was still a lot of chatter, mostly about who could be considered the greatest goalkeeper, Khune or Meyiwa, followed by a lengthy discussion of how women love to complain.

'Women don't know what they want. There's not a creature on earth that's more complicated. There's nothing you'll ever do that will satisfy her,' the guy who was cutting my hair said.

'There's only one thing that shuts a woman up and that's money. For as long as you're poor, she'll never respect you,' a man waiting in line said.

'Bo cherrie just wants commitment. You need to show her that you love her and are faithful to her, that's all,' Lolo added his two cents.

'Hayi suka! Just 'cause you're sitting here with your girl-friend, you're talking about being faithful. There's no man who can stay faithful to one woman, uyazi nawe.'

The conversation taking place around me was ironic. It sounded to me like all those guys were complaining. I still loved the feeling of the blade running over my scalp, though. Lolo was right – shaving our heads at the same time was a very cheap date, but strangely romantic.

* * *

We had already circled our entire neighbourhood twice. It was starting to get dark, but I was still not ready to go into the house because of the noise that was coming from inside. Mama and Dineo's voices echoed down the street. Like two bulls locking horns, they battled over me.

'You forget that you brought disgrace to this family by dragging a stomach in at seventeen. Now Naledi is doing the same thing. You are the one who taught her to behave like this. She is out on the streets sleeping with everything that's on two legs!'

'Kanti, what the hell do they teach you in church? How to walk around with your nose in the air and your head in the clouds? How long do you plan on punishing me, Mama? Don't forget that the only reason why Naledi slept on the street is because you locked her out!'

An hour had passed, and the argument had yet to die down. Having heard enough of it, I was about to pull Lolo away to take a walk down to the shops when we heard the sound of glass shattering. I bolted towards the house, with Lolo running close behind me.

Dineo was crouching on the floor, Mama standing a few feet away from her. Mama's chest was rising and dropping. Dineo looked both angry and stunned. My grandfather's photograph was on the floor, covered in pieces of broken glass.

'This is all you, Naledi. You and that boy standing behind you, you have torn down the walls of your grandfather's house!' Mama marched past Lolo and me to the bedroom.

When I returned an hour later from walking outside with Lolo, Mama was still lamenting. My feet led me straight to the bedroom. I didn't stop to contemplate what I was doing. Mama was on her knees with her arms and head raised. Her tongue was moving rapidly and there was sweat dripping down her neck.

'Mama, please stop it,' I said loudly enough to halt her prayer.

She sprang to her feet, with an energy unlike that of any woman her age. Her eyes were wide and her mouth hung open.

'Stop it,' I said in a low voice, but firmly.

It took my grandmother a few seconds to shake herself out of her shock. She pointed towards the door and bellowed, 'Get out, Satan!'

I felt my heart pounding in my chest, but I was not going to run. I was not going to allow my fear to silence me any longer.

'I said get out!' Mama's entire body vibrated. I shuddered. I took a breath and went to sit on the bed. Dineo swung open the bedroom door, panicked. My brazen behaviour had paralysed my grandmother. She stood staring at me as if she were truly seeing the devil himself.

'That's my mother.' I pointed at Dineo who stood in the doorway, before turning back to face my grandmother. 'I don't care how or what she did, but that is my mother and she kept me when others would have chosen otherwise.' I took a deep breath. 'And I love Lolo, Mama. You're a woman – you know very well what that feels like.'

In the stillness I could hear rain begin to fall. I continued: 'You have done all you can to love and protect me, but please, Mama, stop holding on so tight.'

I left the room and sat crying on the bathroom floor. That night I slept next to Dineo in the living room.

* * *

It seemed as though the mystical power that had rested in the Balobedu Queen Modjadji had found its way to Johannesburg. There was no thunder and no lightning, just showers cooling down a city that had been dealt blistering heat over the last couple of weeks. Dineo and I sat at the table gossiping like two teenage girls over brown porridge.

'So, Naledi, tell me, what does Zola teach you again?'

'Zola? Who's Zola?'

'Bathong, Naledi, the guy who drops you off every day.'

'Oh, you mean Mthi.'

'Yes, him. His name is Zola, Mthi is his surname, akere.'

'Oh, I'm sorry, I didn't know you were already on a first-name basis with the guy.'

'Mxm, o tla swaba!'

My mother and I were still giggling when Mama walked in. She pulled out a chair and sat down. After a few minutes of eating in a room where everyone seemed too afraid to move or even cough, Mama sent Dineo and me into complete shock.

'So what is the name of this drama you are doing?'

I must have been imagining this. There was no way my grandmother was talking to me after the night we had had, especially not about the play.

'Naledi, what is the name of the play?' Mama asked again.

'*So-phia-town*,' I said with hesitation.

'Mmmh . . .' Mama nodded.

Five minutes passed. Then ten minutes. The longer we sat there in silence, the more I felt myself burning up. I wanted to get up to open the door, but Mama would have thought I was crazy to allow a cool breeze in while it was raining.

'So, the thing of you becoming a doctor is now out of the window?'

I looked at Dineo, who understood my confusion.

'Mama, Naledi ke actress,' said Dineo. 'She has never in her life said she wants to be a doctor.'

'Helang, Dineo, don't limit this child. There are not a lot of people in this community that go to university. Naledi has options!'

While Dineo and Mama continued to go back and forth, there was a knock on the door.

'Ko ko, Naledi!'

My heart started racing when I heard Lolo's voice. I gulped

down the last spoon of porridge and by the time I had placed my bowl in the sink, Dineo was already at the door. My grandmother glared at him.

'Oh, we were just eating. Would you like to come in?' said Dineo.

'No, no, it's fine. I need to get going anyway otherwise I'll be late for school.'

I didn't understand how Dineo thought that Lolo's sitting at the table with us over breakfast would be a good idea. And I also didn't understand why Lolo would think showing up at my grandmother's door was not a problem.

'Lolo, wa gafa!' I yelled at him on our trek to the taxis.

'Uh jo phela, I have to romance you now and hit you with surprises every now and again.'

'So your idea of romance is getting me into trouble?'

'You want me to let you walk alone in the rain after you told me yourself that you're scared of the rain?'

'I'm not scared of rain, jo. How can a person be scared of rain? I said I'm scared of lightning – there's a difference!'

We approached the long queue where all those who commute to town waited for the taxis. I found my favourite window seat in the last row. Lolo pulled out a box of Lindt chocolates and passed them through the window. He stuck his head in, and I leaned over and kissed him.

'Good luck, baby,' he said, winking at me.

I blushed at the looks the other passengers were passing in my direction.

'Mxm!' one woman sucked her teeth.

All day long, the rain did not cease its onslaught. I prayed that those rain blessings were meant for myself and the rest of my cast, who began to trickle into the theatre that afternoon.

I could feel my anxiety rise when a WhatsApp from Minnie came in:

Break a leg, friend. And why didn't you tell us that bae is bringing the in-laws 🙈 😅.

It was showtime. The stage lights came up and the curtain opened.

Everything I had fought for – it all came down to that single moment. And we performed as if performing were oxygen itself. At the end, the applause was so overwhelming it left me shaking from the euphoria and relief that was flowing through my body. I stared into the crowd, my eyes fixed on my grandmother's face. She had actually come. Unlike Dineo and Kedi, who were the loudest two people in the audience – 'Yessss, Naledi, yeessssss!' they shouted – Mama was quiet and still. She was the only person in the theatre who remained seated. She looked at me in a way that transported me back to the days when she was still my whole world and I was hers. I cried as Mama's tears fell onto her cheeks. I knew she would never say it out loud, but Mama was proud of me.

Acknowledgements

Firstly, I thank God for choosing me to be the vessel through which this story is told. To my parents and my brothers, thank you for providing a safe space for me to evolve as a woman, and as a creative being. My beloved grandmothers, Gertrude, Nancy and Minah, thank you for your friendship, your wisdom and for continuously holding up the walls of our family.

To my late grandmother Dolly (Norah), I hope this small tribute is well-received where you are. To walk this life with four strong matriarchs has shifted the way I see the world.

To Nobantu and Thuli, I could never put in words how much your love means to me. You have always been there to catch my tears when they fall. Reti and Tshepo, thank you for your constant support, towards me and this entire family. Thabi, Lerato, Zweli, Thato and Olwi, you bring light to my life.

To my mentor, Angela Briggs, who in such a short space of time taught me so much about writing. I'm so grateful for you. We did it! To the entire Jakes Gerwel Foundation family – Theo, Suzette, Miriam, Audrey, Deidre and Zama – thank you for making me a better writer with each workshop and dinner table conversation. Letuka Dlamini, I will never forget that you are the only person who read my badly written first draft. I took your feedback very seriously, thank you. To my friends Didie, Melissa and my wolfpack, thank you for growing with me and celebrating each milestone with me.

Lastly, thank you Stevlyn for seeing my gifts and believing in Naledi, so much so that you have helped carry me over the finish line. Thank you to the Kwela team for making this happen.

Lebohang Mazibuko
June 2021